We decided on seven o'clock as the time to make the call. I had checked to see what was on television at that time in case there was a program that might appeal to Craig. I didn't want him instantly irritated by getting a phone call in the midst of watching something fascinating. The TV schedule was blah.

I went home and washed my hair thoroughly. It couldn't have been cleaner. I was all set.

No I wasn't. I was terrified. What did I really know about Craig except what he looked like? I knew that almost everybody liked him. Whenever I heard kids talk about him, I mentally collected their adjectives: "friendly," "neat," "great." So now I was picturing friendly, neat, great, *unsuspecting* Craig sitting at home while two master schemers got ready to unleash their master scheme on him. One master schemer. It was all up to me. What would he do when I called? Would he think I was nuts? Would he be right?

MARJORIE SHARMAT was born and raised in Portland, Maine, and now lives with her husband and children in Tucson, Arizona. She is the author of many books for young readers, including *I Saw Him First*, which is also available in a Dell Laurel-Leaf edition.

ALSO AVAILABLE IN LAUREL-LEAF BOOKS:

HOW TO MEET A GORGEOUS GIRL,
  Marjorie Sharmat
HOW TO HAVE A GORGEOUS WEDDING,
  Marjorie Sharmat
I SAW HIM FIRST, *Marjorie Sharmat*
HE NOTICED I'M ALIVE . . . AND OTHER
  HOPEFUL SIGNS, *Marjorie Sharmat*
ROMANCE IS A RIOT, *Joan Winslow*
WHAT IF THEY SAW ME NOW, *Jean Ure*
SEE YOU THURSDAY, *Jean Ure*
WHO LOVES SAM GRANT?, *Delores Beckman*
TENDER BEGINNINGS, *Stuart Buchan*
RESTLESS NIGHTS, *Stuart Buchan*

HOW TO MEET
A Gorgeous Guy

MARJORIE SHARMAT

LAUREL-LEAF BOOKS bring together under a single imprint outstanding works of fiction and nonfiction particularly suitable for young adult readers, both in and out of the classroom. Charles F. Reasoner, Professor Emeritus of Children's Literature and Reading, New York University, is consultant to this series.

Published by
Dell Publishing Co., Inc.
1 Dag Hammarskjold Plaza
New York, New York 10017

Laurel-Leaf Library ® TM 766734, Dell Publishing Co., Inc.
YOUNG LOVE ® is a trademark of DC COMICS INC.

ISBN: 0-440-93553-9

RL: 6.1

Printed in the United States of America
October 1983
10 9 8 7 6 5

For my sons,
ANDREW and CRAIG,
with love

HOW TO MEET
A Gorgeous Guy

1

Ever wanted to be famous? I mean, *really* famous. So famous that you have on your payroll at least a dozen slobbering yes-men who lie to you regularly and rob you blind?

I'm not smart enough or talented enough or lucky enough ever to be that kind of famous. But my cousin, Lisa Blakely, is. She's a scheme a minute, and I'm part of her latest.

I'm about to go out with the "gorgeous guy." It's part of Lisa's scheme. In thirty-five minutes, if he's on time, "gorgeous guy" will arrive at my door to take me out. He is not only gorgeous, he is smart, witty, popular, and a bunch of other things I pretend to disdain because they don't apply to me. Even so, *I* picked him out and he is taking *me* out. I would feel better about this if he actually knew

1

me, had met me, or had *any* kind of face-to-face contact with me. What if he runs away when he sees me? I hope he remembers my name. Shari Stapleton isn't the easiest name to remember, but he only learned it yesterday, so there's hope.

What should I wear? I spent all afternoon buying new clothes. But I'm not wearing any of them because new clothes always make me nervous. What if they itch, rip, sag, or contain tags not visible to the wearer but easy to read by everybody else? I don't need any additions of high anxiety to my night.

I don't have to ask myself how I got into this, because I know. When you have a cousin like Lisa, you simply get pushed into things. Lisa is only fifteen, but she is anxious to make it to the top. The top of what remains to be seen, but she wants to be famous and successful as soon as possible, and maybe sooner than possible. She is always on the lookout for opportunities. She does not believe in working your way up, studying your way up, building one step at a time. Lisa believes in big leaps. In the privacy of my own head I refer to her as Big Leap Lisa, and I'm afraid I'll get really mad at her someday and spill it. I think that Lisa will grow up to be either incredibly successful or a huge failure. She might land on the cover of *Newsweek* or *Business Life* as the nation's youngest successful entrepreneur. On the other hand, I can also see her peddling windup toy monkeys on street corners.

Lisa sucked me into her newest "opportunity" merely by saying "Hey, read this." We were walking home from school last week and Lisa was reading one of those junky magazines that you pretend not to read at the supermarket while you take in every word on the front cover. Lisa buys them and doesn't even turn around to see if any of the kids have seen her do it.

Lisa was pointing to an ad.

> Are you a teenager? If so, D & B Press is looking for *your* fresh and innovative ideas to help launch our premiere issue of *Acne Magazine*. And, yes, we pay!
> Call us today.

There was a telephone number and something about their being an equal opportunity employer.

"Okay, I read it," I said to Lisa. "It means nothing to me because I don't have any fresh or innovative ideas. Even if I did, I wouldn't give them to a magazine that can't even spell its own name. *Acme* is spelled *A-C-M-E*. It sounds boring, but *Acne Magazine* sounds ridiculous. It should be published by the Pimple Press."

"Laugh," said Lisa. "You never recognize opportunity, anyway."

"This is opportunity?"

"Staring you straight in the eye," said Lisa. "Did you see 'premiere issue'? We're talking new; we're talking first. When you're first, you've got the best chance. And I've got plenty of ideas."

"Do you really want to be a writer?"

"Writer, rock star, international business tycoon —something along those lines."

When we got to Lisa's house, I went in with her. We hang out together so much that we hardly ever ask "Want to come in?" We just follow each other, go places together, split, get back together, without formal invitations or announcements. I think we're like dogs that way. I also think we have one of those relationships where she thinks she's putting up with me and my faults and I think I'm putting up with her and her faults and we're both right.

"I'm calling D and B Press," she said, and she went to the phone.

"So fast?"

"Fast? The line's probably busy already," she said. "I've probably lost out. Hello? D and B?" Lisa looked at me and shook her head affirmatively. "My name is Lisa Blakely," she said into the receiver. "I read your ad and I've always, always wanted to be a magazine writer. Ideas are my speciality. Especially teenage ideas that are fresh and innovative. That's why I'm answering your ad. You're a New York City publisher, right? I live in the suburbs and I live a really teenage life. And I'm particularly interested in making an idea affiliation with a New York publisher. So when can we get together and talk about all of this?"

Instinctively I wanted to cover my eyes, although it was my ears that were picking up all this bull.

"Yes, I *could*. Are you open Saturdays? Or I could come after school on a weekday."

Lisa was jumping up and down while she carried on this conversation.

"Next Monday? Fine. Let me just write down your address." Lisa got busy writing something. She keeps pad and pencil by her phone. That's the way she is. "Is that in Greenwich Village or The Bronx?" she asked. "I'm not quite familiar with your street. Oh, the *Village*, of course. Three P.M.? Good. See you then."

Lisa hung up and started to leap around the room. "I'm on my way," she said.

"To where and what?"

"You heard it. I've got an appointment with D and B Press, magazine publishers with offices in New York City."

"You mean you've got an appointment with a

5

total stranger. This could be a pornography ring or something, advertising for teenagers with ideas. I wonder what kind of ideas they really want."

"You're great company, Shari. You're messing up my big moment, did you know that? What you just heard could be one of those momentous conversations recalled years later when I'm at the top, remembering how it all started."

"It could also be an invitation to get ripped off, assaulted, or violated in a manner as yet undreamed of. . . ."

Suddenly Lisa looked deflated. "Do you really think so? The lady on the phone—it was a lady—sounded okay, not kinky or anything. Kind of professional, you know. What should I do? If I don't keep that appointment, I'll never forgive myself. Okay, don't say it. If I do keep that appointment, I may never forgive myself."

"Okay, I won't say it," I said.

Lisa brightened. "*You* come with me. We'll be safe, the two of us."

I had two choices. Yes. Or no. If I had said no, I would not be getting ready to go out with "gorgeous guy."

2

I get a so-so allowance, and I blew a week's worth on my transportation into and around New York City that Monday afternoon. Lisa was treating me for the trip home. After we got to Grand Central Station we caught a bus downtown to Greenwich Village. It would have been helpful if Lisa had asked directions about getting to the so-called offices of D & B Press. But Lisa likes to pretend she knows things she doesn't know. She had a rough idea of where we were going because she had opened a couple of street maps.

Have you ever looked for an address and found yourself in a very charming neighborhood that slowly but relentlessly gets seedier and seedier? That's how it was when we were looking for D & B

Press. When we reached ultimate seedy, something inside me said that we were there. Sure enough, we went into a building where there was a hand-lettered D & B PRESS sign downstairs, which also stated that D & B was five flights up. The stairs were narrow and littered.

"Isn't this atmospheric?" Lisa said bravely.

On the fifth floor the door to D & B Press was slightly ajar. I peeked inside. "Don't peek!" said Lisa. "That's so juvenile."

Lisa pushed the door open and we walked into a large room with peeling paint and cracks all over the walls. Partitioned off at the front of the room was a cubicle with a desk, a telephone, a chair, and two absolutely beautiful plants that gave you the impression someone humane but bereft of funds might be masterminding the decor. The large room looked like a combined living room and office with one stuffed chair, one lamp, and a desk covered with papers. There were posters among the cracks on the wall.

Also there was a bad smell. It probably came from the pizza crusts and opened wine bottles on the floor.

"Wild!" whispered Lisa.

"Sleazy," I whispered back.

"Hello!" A guy in jeans and no shoes and a T-shirt that had YOU CAN LIVE WITH ACNE on the front suddenly appeared beside us. Beside him was a lady, also barefoot, wearing the kind of peasant outfit that peasants donate to charities.

I wanted to leave. But Lisa looked pleased. After all, we were in a magazine publisher's office, weren't we? Lisa equated eccentric clothing and behavior with creative genius when it appeared in the right surroundings. I knew that if these same two characters had approached her on the street, she would have fled in panic.

"Come in," said the guy. "I'm Derek and this is Bonita." No last names.

Bonita sort of grunted. She was older than Derek. Somewhere between thirty and sixty, I guessed. I'm not good at ages.

"I'm your three o'clock appointment, Lisa Blakely," said Lisa. "And this is Shari Stapleton, my assistant."

I let that pass.

Derek motioned us to sit down. That presented a problem. There was one chair in the cubicle, one in the living room, and four people. Derek sat down on the floor and so did Bonita. I pulled up the cubicle chair, and Lisa sat down in the stuffed chair.

I stared at Derek. Sitting on the floor in his jeans and T-shirt, he looked young and disreputable. He looked like one of those guys who run away from home in the middle of high school, leaving his parents forever wondering what happened. This is what happened to him. Peeling walls, strange odors, and Bonita. I wondered if the entire neighborhood was full of dropouts. I could see armies of parents descending to claim their lost kids, then taking one look, and changing their collective minds.

Derek said, "As you see, we're *very* new. Not even set up yet. Not that we'll ever be *The New Yorker*...."

"We don't *want* to be *The New Yorker*," said Bonita.

"We're going to be the thinking teenager's magazine," said Derek. "We're anticorporation, antiplastic, anticliché."

And prodirt, I was thinking.

"We'll be fresh, involved, innovative, and very upfront with teenagers. That's why we're calling our magazine *Acne!*"

Lisa looked at me. It wasn't a misprint. Acne was on purpose.

Derek said, "We're going to make *Acne* a household word."

"It already is," I said.

Lisa gave me a dirty look. She seemed impressed by everything. She said to Derek, "That's a very honest name. So many teenagers do have acne. I get it now and then, but just on my chin. I'm one of the fortunate ones."

I'm not, so I kept my mouth shut.

Derek stood up and went to the desk. He picked up a bunch of papers.

"Here," he said, holding the papers in front of Lisa and me. "This is a paste-up of our first issue." He started turning pages.

I leaned over for a better look. The pages looked professional and well designed. I couldn't believe it.

"We *are* a real honest-to-goodness magazine. That is, we soon will be," said Derek. "I know our offices aren't beautiful, but we're cutting corners and putting our capital into this magazine. We have subscribers. We have advertisers."

"We're clever people," Bonita grunted. "Aren't we, son?"

Son? They were mother and son. Maybe he *was* a high school dropout and Mom had found him and decided to move in and keep an eye on him.

Derek went on. "Our magazine is ready to go, but we feel that something is missing. That we should have an article from a teenager's point of view. Something that tells us what's important to a teenager." Derek turned to Lisa. "I imagine you've come equipped with tons of fresh ideas. You sounded so bubbly over the telephone."

Ideas. That's what this meeting was all about. Did Lisa have any? When I asked her on the train coming in, she had said "Sure," but she didn't say anything more. So I didn't ask. Lisa wanted to leap to the top all by herself.

"I *am* bubbly," said Lisa, which I thought was courageous, considering the surroundings. "I've been doing some research on what makes certain magazines and articles popular."

Bonita grunted, "We're not imitative."

Derek smiled an oily smile. "But we're *listening*, aren't we, Mom?"

"Yeah," grunted Bonita.

"Well, some things are *basic*," said Lisa, "and you just can't ignore that. For example, you eat, don't you. And I eat. But *I'm* not imitating *you*."

Derek looked at Lisa with admiration. So did I. Lisa wasn't bad, not bad at all. Maybe she wouldn't end up selling monkeys on street corners.

Bonita grunted.

Lisa kept going. "Just because somebody else does something doesn't mean it's invalidated. The biggest thing around right now is 'how-to.' How to do this, how to do that. Teenagers always want to know how to be more popular. And *that's* my article idea. How to be more popular."

Bonita practically snarled. "Popularity is like

plastic. It's like corporations. It doesn't belong in *Acne*. It has no soul. It would be a violation of everything that *Acne* is going to stand for."

"It would sell copies," said Lisa positively.

Lisa definitely won't be selling monkeys on street corners.

"Whoa, Mom!" said Derek. "We've got to catch our readers early on or there won't be any readers. Isn't that on target, Lisa?"

"On target," said Lisa.

"And yet . . ." said Derek.

"Yet what?" asked Lisa.

"Popularity is such an abstraction. Cigar?" Derek took a cigar out of his pocket. From the bottom of the pocket, since it had a hole in it.

"I don't smoke," said Lisa. "Anything."

Derek handed the cigar to Bonita. She handed it back. Derek put it back in his pocket, through the bottom. "I'm afraid that popularity is a terribly vague thing, sweetie. Teenagers like specifics. Could you be more specific?"

"Popularity means getting guys if you're a girl and getting girls if you're a guy," said Lisa.

"We anticipate having a large female readership," said Derek.

"Then, you'd want guys," said Lisa. "Like how to get a gorgeous guy."

"Crass," said Bonita.

"But promising," said Derek. "Maybe we could soften it a bit."

"It's hard to *meet* a gorgeous guy," I said. Why was I butting in?

"But aren't you surrounded by guys at school?" asked Derek.

"Yeah," I said. "But if they're not in your class or in a club you belong to or in your neighborhood or something, then you can't meet them."

Lisa looked at me angrily. I was sorry I had gotten into this.

But Derek was pleased. "I think we have it," he said. He turned to Lisa. "How to *meet* a gorgeous guy."

"What do I do?" asked Lisa. "List one hundred and one ways to meet one?"

"No, sweetie," said Derek. "Let me tell you something about the magazine business. You have to personalize things. You have to write something readers individually will identify with. For instance, what if, say, an average sort of girl wanted to meet a gorgeous guy. How would she go about it?"

"A case history," said Bonita. "You've heard of them?"

I had. You get them in hospitals and prisons.

Lisa was excited. "You accept my idea?" she

asked, conveniently forgetting that it was partially my idea.

"Yes," said Derek. "Provided you can come up with an average sort of girl and a gorgeous guy and arrange for them to meet."

"Oh," said Lisa. "That sounds hard."

"We pay," said Derek. "And your name gets into our magazine."

"How much?" asked Lisa. She was really down to business.

"As much as two hundred dollars," said Derek.

"And as little as?" asked Lisa. Boy, she was great.

Derek didn't lose his cool. "One hundred dollars if we accept your article but we're not absolutely wild about it."

"I can do it," said Lisa. "There are at least six gorgeous guys I know of."

"And your average girl?" asked Derek. "We need someone *very* average. Let me tell you something about average. Parents try to tell their kids they're special when they're really average. But average is what makes the world go round. Let's face it. Average is where it's at."

Derek was looking directly at me.

So was Bonita.

So was Lisa.

3

I agreed to be average because I was anxious to leave. At the time I didn't think about meeting a gorgeous guy as a *real* reality. Maybe Lisa would change her mind on the way home, when she was no longer intoxicated by the smells of moldy pizza crusts and wine turned to vinegar. And if she didn't change her mind, how could she actually arrange a meeting, anyway?

Derek and Lisa discussed some last-minute average-gorgeous details while I got up and pretended to read the posters. It was sticky to be talked about like that. Lisa promised to have the entire project finished within two weeks. Two weeks? She gave Derek her telephone number and said she'd be giving him progress reports.

"Remember, Mom and I will be here to give you support," said Derek.

Suddenly I had a question for either Mom or Son. "Will *my* name be in the magazine?"

"Only if you want it to and sign a release," said Derek. "Otherwise we'll probably call you . . ."

"Penelope," said Bonita, as if that were the one and only name possible.

"Never fear. We won't call you Ms. Average or anything nauseatingly adorable like that," said Derek.

When we finally got outside, the fresh air seemed awfully fresh. Maybe that's not an original kind of observation, but *I'm* not planning to be a writer.

We started to walk. "I'm not going to do it," I said.

"What do you mean you're not going to do it?" asked Lisa. "You *said* you were going to do it."

"It was an insane thing to say. Everything was insane in there. The peeling walls, *Acne*, Derek, Bonita. . . . I was in the mood for insane."

"Okay. Okay. I'll get another average person. You think you're the only average person around? Don't do me any favors. There are plenty of girls out there just dying to meet a gorgeous guy. Remember, the project is gorgeous. Not just anybody. Maybe I'll ask Eve."

17

"Eve Raines?"

Lisa knew I didn't like Eve. Eve was nasty and sly. She was way above average that way. Actually she wasn't average in any way you could think of. Lisa was needling me.

"Lisa, think about this. *Think!* We had a nice little adventure. A little creepy and tacky and weird, but it was almost fun. I could even get fond of Derek and Bonita if I'm exposed to them long enough. Five, six, maybe seven years. But I'm your cousin and I'm your friend. And I'm telling you that you could get all involved in this gorgeous guy project and who says they're going to publish your story? Who says they're going to pay you? Maybe if we went back there right now we'd find they were gone, cleared out. Not that there was much to clear out. Maybe it's a con game. I haven't figured out the angle. They're like from a dream. Ever see one of those movies where the hero is with some people in their house and then he goes back to the very same house the next day and there isn't a trace of the people or their belongings from the day before or any clue that they had ever been there? Spooky. Maybe Derek and Bonita are extraterrestrial."

Lisa had been listening intently to everything I said. She answered, "You just don't want to be average, do you?"

I walked faster. No use arguing with Big Leap

Lisa. I wondered if she'd really ask Eve Raines. How could she do that to me? I had to think affirmatively. Maybe Derek and Bonita were legitimate, sincere, sane. What if Project Gorgeous Guy just happened to be a success? What if Eve, instead of me, lived happily ever after, or even for a few weeks, knowing she had a gorgeous guy in her life.

There was something Lisa didn't know about me. Something no one knew about me. There *was* a gorgeous guy I wanted to meet. For a year I'd wanted to meet him, even though I gave up after the first six months when nothing happened. His name: Craig Andrew. His occupation: Making Me Feel Depressed Because I Couldn't Meet Him. I was also depressed thinking about what wouldn't happen after I met him. He was a senior. Everything about him was intense. His eyes and expression and his jaw. I go for intense. So do most of the girls in school. Craig used to date a girl from another school, a lucky Inez something or other. I saw her with him a few times. She giggles and she's an arm clutcher. Lately I've seen him with a beautiful senior, Rosalind Rothman. I'm not jealous of her because everything's too remote for jealousy. What difference does it make whether she's going out with Craig or not? I mean, if she didn't, I still couldn't.

But boy, I'd like to!

I looked at Lisa. Maybe, like Lisa, I should think of situations as being opportunities.

"I'll do this for you," I said. "I'll be your average person. You arrange for me to meet the gorgeous guy."

Lisa stopped and gave me a little hug. "Oh, Shari, you won't regret it. Thank you, thank you!"

"You're welcome."

"I don't want to rush you or anything, Shari, but could you start thinking about the particular guy you'd like to meet. If you don't come up with anybody, I'll get a bunch of school yearbooks and we can go over them. Unless you'd like to pick out a random stranger around school. That would be a big challenge."

"I'll try to think of someone," I said. "I just have to point my mind in the right direction."

"I wish you could think of somebody instantly so we could start plotting right on the train home. Wouldn't that be fun!"

"Don't rush me."

"Can I throw a few names at you in case you know who they are?"

"Well, okay. But try seniors."

"Why seniors?"

"Because I'm a sophomore and older is better. So let's start alphabetically with seniors."

"First name alphabetically or last name?"

"Last name."

Lisa only had to go through two names before she reached Craig Andrew. I hoped I didn't sound too anxious when I said "Stop right there."

4

It was after six when I got home, but the only sign of supper was a casserole my brother, Milton, had taken out of the freezer and placed on the counter. Milton is only ten, but he has this casserole job when my mother and I aren't available. On Sundays Mom makes a week's worth of casseroles and freezes them. Some people would call that being organized. I call it being monotonous. Milton is supposed to remember to take the casserole-of-the-day out of the freezer and then heat it up. He also tosses salads. He's a good kid, and only occasionally a pest.

This is my family situation. I live with my mother and Milton. My father divorced Mom five years ago so he could marry a very dumpy-looking lady, Gloria Jean Dumont, who has bags under her eyes so dark they look like they are holding the world's supply of tea. She has a crack in her voice that would sound sexy if it went with another face. Her conversations all sound like they're coming out of a police car radio. She looks old enough to be my father's mother, except that my father's mother recently had a face-lift and now she looks younger than Gloria Jean.

Since my mother is attractive, you'd think there was something wrong with her personality that made my father leave. But there isn't. Great people get run out on. Mostly by weak people, I think. My father lives three states away, and now and then he comes to visit us. It makes my mother tense, but she puts up with it because of Milton and me. It makes us tense too, but your father is your father. He always brings Gloria Jean along and they stick around for two weeks. They stay in a fancy hotel, and Tea Bags does a lot of shopping in the city. She's rich because of her first husband.

I put the casserole in the oven. Milton doesn't like to put it in the oven directly from the freezer. That means it can sit out for hours and hours. Then I went to Mom's Designer Room. Mom designs clothes for women under the SHARI label. Named after me, of course. She got started when she made a dress for me to wear to a birthday party when I was six years old. She designed a tiny creature on it that she made from scraps of material. I don't know what the creature was supposed to be, but if you cross a giraffe with an owl with a snake, you've got it. Well, everybody was nuts about the dress, and Mom got requests to make some for other little girls. The only trouble was that the girls outgrew some of the dresses before Mom finished them. So Mom turned to grown-up stuff. She still uses the same emblem. It's on her label with the name SHARI. So I have a little bit of local fame because my name is sewn inside some of the richest necks in town. The women in our town seem to like their SHARIs. Mom's outfits are one of a kind, and she charges lots of money. "But not enough," the accountant, Gabriel, always says, as he pores over the books.

"Hi, Mom."

Mom looked up from her sketchpad. It was such a familiar sight—Mom looking up from her sketchpad. It was my favorite view of Mom. My next favorite was of her and Gabriel going over the books. It was business, but it looked domestic. The only thing that spoiled it was the knowledge that Gabriel charges by the hour.

Mom seemed a little tired. When you work at home, you never get free from work. Also, you can't tell the difference between being at home and being at work.

She sniffed. "Oh, you put the casserole in. Thanks. So, how was your trip into the city?"

"Okay," I said. I didn't think I should tell Mom about Derek and Bonita. As unwholesome as they were in person, telling about them would make them seem even more unwholesome. Derek had a ratty kind of charm that you can't recapture in words.

"Do anything special?"

"Well . . ."

The doorbell rang. "Is Gabriel coming for supper?" I asked.

"Who else," said Mom. "And then it's another session with the books."

Mom washed up. I washed up. And Milton let Gabriel in. With a name like Gabriel you'd think *he* was the dress designer. Gabriel isn't married, and he eats supper with us a couple of times a week. There is a lot of talk about receipts and interest rates and write-offs and tight money at the supper table. Mom has been in the dress-designing business for eight years, and she is still trying, with Gabriel's help, to figure out if she's making any money. I know that Gabriel is because, as I mentioned, he charges by the hour. I'm not an accountant, but I figure that Mom is making money because Dad hardly ever sends anything and we haven't gone from middle class to poor.

Mom changed her outfit for Gabriel. She always changes when he comes over, no matter how tired she is. That's why I figure she thinks of him as a boyfriend.

It's strange to have a mother who has a *boyfriend*. I mean, that's what girls my age have or are hoping to have. But my own mother! I used to think that once you got married, the boyfriend business was over and done with. My mother didn't go looking for Gabriel as a boyfriend and he didn't go looking for her. The Yellow Pages brought them together. I would hate to meet a guy through the Yellow Pages. What happened was that last year my mother decided she needed someone to help with the business end of her designing business. She found Gabriel listed in the phone book under ACCOUNTANTS. She went to his office, and then he started to show up at our house. For a while I just thought of him as somebody temporary, like a repairman who performs a service and leaves. But Gabriel showed up more and more often. Mom's business isn't *that* big. Gabriel could have done all the figures for General Motors and IBM in the time he spent with Mom. I began to think of him as a *man,* the first man to regularly come to our house since my father left. This changed the whole picture for me. I've never felt

26

threatened by accountants. But a man who was interested in my mother was something else.

One night Gabriel came to take my mother *out* to the movies. A date. I watched them walk out the door, just the way my mother used to walk out with my father. Mom was all scented up in her going-out perfume, and she was all done up in one of her new designs. Gabriel must have doused himself in shaving lotion or cologne because together they sort of reeked. Gabriel had left his briefcase at home, and he didn't look anything like his usual conservative self. In fact, he was wearing a plaid jacket that was probably supposed to show how macho he could look. I think it showed how insecure he was, to get talked into buying a bad joke. But what really got to me was that Mom and Gabriel were trying so hard to make a good impression on each other. They *cared*.

After they left, Milton walked in. "I sniffed both of them three rooms away," he said.

"You noticed, too?"

"How could I miss it? Do you think Gabriel is a chemist in his spare time? He smelled like a lab." Milton laughed.

"What are you laughing about?" I asked. I was angry. "I think he's taking Dad's place."

"Dad doesn't have a place," Milton said.

For a minute I couldn't answer. I was stunned by what Milton said. I was also stunned that he, a ten-year-old, was smarter than I was.

Milton plopped down on the floor, which he likes to do when he anticipates a long conversation. And especially when he thinks he has something clever to contribute.

"Dad went off and married somebody else," he said. "If Gabriel's here or isn't here, Dad's still split. There's no connection, see?"

"I guess."

"Don't you like Gabriel? What if you met him, all by himself, like Mom did through the Yellow Pages? What if he were just an accountant and not Mom's boyfriend?"

"Well, he's a nice guy. But Mom pays him, and people you pay money to are usually nice to you."

"But he *works* for her. He should get paid."

Milton was sounding cocky. In a way I wanted to end this conversation, but in a way I wanted to keep it going. "You've been thinking about this in that ten-year-old head of yours, haven't you?" I said. "And you've got all the answers. So what are they?"

"Let's make a deal. How much are they worth to you? Pay me, or I'll keep silent forever."

"Milton, I'm going to clobber you."

"Okay. Mom's happy about Gabriel. She lights

up when he's around. Mom the candle. I think that's great. And that's it."

"What if he walks out on her like Dad did?"

"Are you kidding? He was trying so hard tonight to make her like him. He looked like a collision of rainbows. He smelled like a lab. He's wacko over her."

I bent down and hugged Milton. I was his big sister. I was supposed to help him, not the other way around.

5

Milton treats Gabriel like a pal, and Gabriel enjoys it.

"What's new, Gabe?" asked Milton as we all sat down at the table.

"What's new with you, Milt?" Gabriel asked as he took a *very* small portion of casserole. Every time he took a very small portion, which happened to be every time, I figured that was proof he liked Mom. He hated her food. You'd have to be an idiot not to notice that. So if the food wasn't the attraction, what was left? Gabriel lives with his mother, by the way. So he's able to get plenty of home cooking at home. Milton thinks it's awful that Gabriel lives with his mother. That's the only thing Milton thinks is awful about Gabriel.

Milton and Gabriel found out what was new

with each other. Then I asked, "How much money does it cost to start a magazine, Gabriel?"

I don't know why I asked. Maybe I was looking for a clue about Derek and Bonita.

"Are you thinking of starting one?" asked Gabriel, smiling. Gabriel has a precise smile and a precise face and a precise build. All very good things for an accountant to have for his image.

"When I get a million dollars," I answered. "Would it cost something like that to start a magazine?"

"It all depends," said Gabriel.

When you hear "it all depends" and then you hear what it all depends *upon*, that takes you clear through supper and the dessert Gabriel brought.

Gabriel was trying hard to be precise and accurate, but "cash flow" always turns me off, and I started to daydream about Craig Andrew again.

What if I met him all by myself? Without any help from Lisa. What if I telephoned him, just like that, that very night? It would be all over with, for better or for worse. But my hair wasn't washed, so I didn't want to do it. I have telephone insecurity. I always think the person on the other end of the line can see me, even though I know that's not possible with my present telephone equipment. But I can't make important calls with dirty hair or in the nude or with my room a mess. This is a handicap that could follow me through life. It might even cost me my life if my house was burning and I was in ripped nightclothes and afraid that I'm not presentable enough to telephone the fire department. Maybe I would make an exception for the fire department, as I think they have seen everything.

Anyway, there I was sitting at the supper table, wondering if I could wash and dry my hair in time to make the call.

"I think I'll wash my hair," I said in the middle of Gabriel's cash flow.

"Are you making an important phone call?" asked Milton.

Sometimes I think Milton knows too much.

I didn't answer. But I finished my meal in a hurry. It was my turn to clean up the kitchen. We take turns, including Milton. It seems fair to me. Anyway, I enjoy thinking while I handle the dishes. We have a dishwasher, but there's lots of scraping to do, and putting things away, and labeling leftovers.

Something was happening to me. Lisa, and even Derek and Bonita, had, if I'm not sounding too dramatic, opened some mental doors for me. They made me want to venture out, to try something. Impossibilities had become possibilities. Maybe what it all came down to was that I really wanted to meet Craig and always had. I deserved to try for something I thought I didn't deserve to try for. If everything failed, I hoped I could go back to the way I was before I started.

By the time I finished in the kitchen, it was too late to wash my hair.

6

There are all kinds of ways to try to meet someone. Some are clever, some are dumb, some are corny, some are gross, some are silly, and most of them don't work.

Lisa drew up a whole list of ideas on how I could meet Craig Andrew.

"Change your religion and go to his church.

"Join the clubs and groups that he joins. For example, try out for the football team, and if they don't take you, complain that they're sexist.

"Switch to his dentist and coordinate his six-month checkups with yours.

"Trip him as he walks by.

"Collapse in his presence."

Lisa seemed very pleased with herself. "Derek

will love these," she said. "And they'll look wonderful in print. So graphic. So upfront."

"Then why don't *you* try them," I said.

"I can't. I'm the author. Besides, I'm not average."

Every time Lisa said average, I cringed a little. I didn't consider it an insult, and I know that Lisa didn't. She's a little weird, but she's not unkind. And to be perfectly honest, *upfront*, I've always considered myself a bit *below* average. I'm one of those not-there, nothing kids. Forgettable is the first descriptive word that comes to mind. I'm the kind of kid people step in front of in lines. Not apologetically, not "Oh, I'm so *sorry*," but as if I were born, nurtured, and exist solely to be stepped in front of. I've always accepted this. I think my ego is healthy. It's probably the same kind of ego that a mouse has, if mice have egos, but that's okay with me. I go out on dates. I'm middlingly popular, because there are a number of mouse-ego guys around and *they* find *me*. But now Lisa was pushing me beyond the boundaries of my mouse ego. I was supposed to meet Craig Andrew, with wonderful things to follow. And there was a backup team, too. Derek and Bonita with their peeling walls and open wine bottles were rooting for me.

"So which one of these ideas would you like to

try?" asked Lisa, as we walked down the hall at school.

"None of the above," I said.

Lisa was angry. "Look," she said. "Are you or aren't you going through with this? Just tell me now. I'll get somebody else if you don't want to do it. You can't keep changing your mind."

"I said I'll do it, and I will."

"How?"

"I'll call Craig Andrew and tell him I'd like to meet him."

"Just like that?"

"Sure."

"Won't he wonder why? You can't say, 'I'd like to meet you because you're gorgeous.' You need an excuse."

"You mean a lie?"

"Well, couldn't you say you're collecting for a charity or something?"

"Are you the charity? Come to think of it, Derek and Bonita could pass for a charity. Maybe I could collect for a third chair for their office."

"Very funny."

Lisa and I walked along silently. Suddenly, up ahead was the object of our project! Craig Andrew.

"Look!" said Lisa. "There he is. Boy, you're lucky. He's something else. You picked a winner."

Craig was walking toward us. Right now, on

the spur of the moment, I could meet him! No planning, no working myself up to it, just now-this-minute and get it over with.

"I'm going to meet him *now*," I said to Lisa.

"Fantastic! What'll you say?"

"I'll think of something."

Craig was now about ten feet away and coming toward us fast. I knew he wouldn't speak to us or even nod because he didn't know us.

"Here goes," I said.

"Wait!" said Lisa. "Look, he's with someone."

Eve Raines caught up to Craig. And I mean caught. She grabbed his arm. Craig must inspire arm grabbers. First Inez, now Eve.

They were passing by us. I heard Eve say something about "Saturday night" and then they were gone.

Lisa and I stopped walking. We moved out of the line of hall traffic and leaned against a wall.

"Well, I guess that's that," she said. "We'll have to pick somebody else. Somebody available."

"Why?"

"*Why?* Because, dear girl, you can't compete with Eve Raines. When a guy is stalked by *sly*, he's lost to the rest of civilization. How about Don Berelson?"

"Not my type," I said.

"Is your head on straight? He's so neat."

"I thought your taste was Derek."

"Funny, funny. You're a riot today. Look, I don't care who you pick. Just pick somebody by tomorrow. The world's the limit."

"Okay," I said. "I'll remember that."

Lisa and I walked to class. I felt deceitful. I had no intention of picking anybody else. When I saw Craig Andrew with Eve Raines, I wanted to meet him more than ever. That made no sense to me, but that's the way it was.

7

I was getting into the spirit of things. I even told Lisa that if I succeeded in meeting "gorgeous guy," *I* wanted the credit in *Acne Magazine*. A little fame never hurt anyone. Why give it to "Penelope"?

And I told Lisa that I wanted to stick with Craig Andrew.

"Are you taking on Eve Raines?" she asked.

"We only saw them together once, and just for a minute," I said.

Lisa turned toward me. "You really like him, don't you? He wasn't just an alphabetical choice, was he?"

"Okay, I admit it. But I never seriously thought about him because he seemed so out of reach. I had my borders and my boundaries and I stuck to them.

If you reach too far, rejection becomes a way of life. But let's not talk about it. Let's act!"

"Good!" Lisa was so excited. "So what'll it be? The football team, the dentist, the church, what?"

"The telephone," I said.

"We're back to that?"

Lisa was disappointed. "It's so unimaginative," she groaned. "Derek expects better than dull from me."

But she didn't put up an argument. Maybe she knew that I was terrified of face-to-face. That the telephone was my way of protecting part of me. And, let's face it, I sound a whole lot better than I look.

"When?" she asked simply.

"Tonight," I said.

"Then hurry home and wash your hair," she said.

"Are you coming over when I make the call?"

"I wouldn't miss it," said Lisa. "I can't miss it. *I'm* what this project is all about. Me and *Acne*."

Lisa wasn't what the project was all about. She was disqualified simply by being nonaverage. But there wasn't any point in making that point, so I let it go.

We decided on seven o'clock as the time to make the call. I had checked to see what was on television at that time in case there was a program that might appeal to Craig. I didn't want him instantly irritated by getting a phone call in the midst of watching something fascinating. The TV schedule was blah.

I went home and washed my hair thoroughly. It couldn't have been cleaner. I was all set.

No I wasn't. I was terrified. What did I really know about Craig except what he looked like? I knew that almost everybody liked him. Whenever I heard kids talk about him, I mentally collected their adjectives: "friendly," "neat," "great." So now I was picturing friendly, neat, great, *unsuspecting* Craig sitting at home while two master schemers got ready to unleash their master scheme on him. One master schemer. It was all up to me. What would he do when I called? Would he think I was nuts? Would he be right?

Maybe he'd be happy to hear from me. He went out with that Inez Arm Clutcher and she wasn't anything special. And so what if I saw him with Rosalind Rothman. Beautiful girls often have severe character defects. I might be the perfect girl for Craig. I might have that combination of elusive qualities that perfume manufacturers always rave about. They never tell you exactly what they are. Men just go crazy over them. I think my voice transmits sexy over the phone. Somebody once told me that when I had laryngitis.

At last I had it straight. A new, mysterious, sexy

voice would be calling Craig Andrew tonight. He'd hardly be able to believe his good luck.

Lisa arrived at seven. I had already looked up and memorized Craig's telephone number. I knew where he lived because there had been an article about his mother in the newspaper a few months ago, and it had said where he lived and the names of his family. His mother is a social worker who runs some sort of clinic for teenagers. She got a big award. At least, the newspaper made it sound big.

As soon as Lisa got to my house, I said "Let's leave."

"What?"

"I want to call from a pay phone," I said.

"You're crazy. Why?"

"I just feel better about it."

"What if he hears coins clinking on the other end? Won't that sound strange?"

"No. It sounds comforting to me. I don't know why. Maybe it all goes with washed hair."

"Hey, that's a good angle for the story. Washed hair, a pay phone."

"Be careful. You're messing around with somebody else's psyche in print."

Lisa and I left the house. "I'm going out," I called to whoever was or wasn't listening.

There was a pay phone five blocks away. Nobody was there. I took some change from my pocket. I had stuffed my pocket full of change. I dropped some coins in the slot and dialed Craig's number. I wondered if I was being disloyal to Lisa to hope very hard that Craig wasn't home. That no one was home. That no one would ever be home at this number.

"Hello."

A girl answered. Craig has a sister. She's a freshman. She looks a lot like Craig, but intense isn't a great look for a girl. So he came out better.

"Is Craig there, please?" Sure enough, it was my voice talking.

"No, but he should be back any minute. Could I have him call you?"

Now what? If I left my name, he might never call me back, and then I wouldn't know if it was deliberate or if my message didn't get delivered. I couldn't call a second time after leaving my name the first time. Then again, if I didn't leave my name, I'd have to call again and my voice would be recognized and he might know I was "the girl who called twice." Maybe three times, if he wasn't home the second time. This must be a common problem for all people afraid to make a certain phone call in the first place. Maybe this would be a good idea for an article in *Acne,* because some teenagers live most of their lives on the telephone.

"Oh, wait a minute, here he comes." Craig's sister had spoken the magic words. Then I heard her say "It's for you, Craig. Some girl."

The way she said "some girl" made me feel like a telephone solicitor. Maybe I was.

"Hello." It was gorgeous guy Craig himself!

"Hello."

Lisa poked me. She knew I had made contact.

It was time for me to say something beyond hello. I said, "My name is Shari Stapleton and I'm a sophomore at Deering High. And you're a senior."

Craig obviously already knew this last piece of information. I went on. "This telephone call isn't a joke. Are we together on that?"

I didn't wait for an answer.

"I come from a liberated family, and we don't think anything of a girl calling a boy. That's why I'm calling you. I'd like to know if you'd like to meet me."

"Shari? Shari . . ." Craig was several sentences back into my spiel. He hadn't gotten past Shari. Who was Shari?

"Do I know you?" he asked. "Do you know me?"

"I've seen you around," I said. "And maybe you've seen me around, but I can't be sure of that."

"What do you look like?"

"Would you please deposit five cents for the

44

next three minutes?" It was the operator, bless her. I dropped a nickel into the slot.

"Are you at a pay phone?" Craig asked. It was better than his last question.

"Yes."

"This call is a joke, correct? I'm kind of busy. It's fun, but I'm busy."

"Then, you don't want to meet me?"

"Meet you? How will I know you? You'll be carrying a machete in your teeth and that's how I'll recognize you, correct?"

"Incorrect. I told you, this isn't a joke. Suddenly I feel as if I know you and I don't want to know you better."

Lisa's eyes widened. She put her hand to her head.

"Wait," said Craig. "I believe you that this isn't a joke. And I'd like to meet you. What did you say your name was?"

"Shari. And now are *you* kidding *me*?"

"No. Are you busy Saturday night?"

"You mean tomorrow night?"

Lisa started dancing around.

"I'm not busy," I said. "I have to sharpen my machete, but that's about my only chore for the evening."

"I'm serious," said Craig.

45

"Me, too." I was wrecking things, I knew. I said, "I'm not busy tomorrow night. I'm totally free."

"Great. Give me your address and I'll pick you up about seven. Okay?"

"Okay. I live at 150-19 25th Drive."

"Got it. See you tomorrow."

"Bye."

Lisa pounced on me the moment I hung up. "That was *wonderful*," she said. "How did you know what to say?"

"It was spontaneous," I said. "If I plan in advance, I just fall apart when the time comes."

"Another good angle for the story," said Lisa. "And a great tip for kids who try to figure out things too much in advance. I bet Derek pays me the whole two hundred dollars."

I had forgotten all about the story and *Acne*.

8

I'm getting ready to meet Craig Andrew. Tonight.
My new clothes are sitting in boxes. I know what
I'm going to wear. A mask, that's what. For face
and body. I feel like hiding my total self. Craig
Andrew is coming over here because he's curious.
Not because he wants to be with *me*. What I've
become is a novelty. I'm what is commonly found
inside a box of Cracker Jacks. Or I can be sent
away for if you enclose the correct number of
coupons or coins or proofs of purchase. You can
find me at carnivals if you win the ring toss. You
can take me home. I *am* a joke.

Milton comes into my room. "Whatcha doing
and where'ya going?" he asks. It's one of his stock
questions.

"I've got a date."

"Who with?"

"Craig Andrew." It sounds great. It sounds like an accomplishment. It is.

"Who's he?"

"A guy."

"You wouldn't kid me, would you?"

"Wise guy."

"Have a real good time, Shari." Milton gives me a kiss. He's like that.

The doorbell rings. No time for a mask. I'm wearing a boring brown outfit. Shirt and skirt. Very nonaggressive-looking, even though it's far too late to be thought of as nonaggressive.

I rush to answer the door. I want to get there before Mom or Milton. I don't want them to find out that I'm going out with someone who doesn't know who I am.

I open the door. Craig is standing there. I had never seen him this close up before. He's wearing a checked jacket. He looks like an ad for a checked jacket. He smiles. Now he looks like an ad for toothpaste. I wonder how it feels to be a walking sales pitch without having to say a word.

He's fantastic! I think of a book I once read by F. Scott Fitzgerald where a man is letting a woman into his place while at the very same moment he's anticipating the sadness of her leaving. That's how I feel about Craig. That's probably because I think of him more in a leaving kind of way than an arriving kind of way.

He looks at me. "Shari?"

It's a serious question. Naturally. Because he doesn't know me. It's so awful. I could be Shari's mother or daughter or sister or anything. I could be hired help. I am a complete stranger. I know he doesn't remember seeing me around school. "Yes," I say. "And you must be Craig." That seems to fit with his asking if I'm Shari, but it's ridiculous because of course I know he's Craig, and I called him up because he's Craig, and that's why he's here.

He doesn't seem to notice that I'm off to a ridiculous start.

I grab my coat, which is a hint that we should leave. Maybe I should invite him in. But I feel weird about it. I yell good-bye to my house, and we leave. His car is parked outside. It's a small car. I don't know car brands. Cars all look the same to me. Either they're big or small. That's it.

He opens the door for me. Polite. I start to climb inside. There is another couple in the back seat! Half the couple is Eve Raines. The other half is Don Berelson.

"We're all going out together, okay?" Craig asks as he sits down behind the wheel. As if I had a choice. Craig introduces me to Eve and Don. I pretend that I don't know who they are. It seems easier that way. Wait till I tell Lisa that I've now met Don Berelson. I know she'll pump me for information, so I try to be alert.

I am also trying to get my present situation straight. Did Craig arrange for Eve and Don to come with us on purpose? Or did he have a date with another girl and this couple, and the girl broke the date? Maybe it was Rosalind. I had heard Eve say something about Saturday night in the hall at school. Was this the Saturday night? I wondered. Is Craig using me as a fill-in? Then again, am I using him? As what, I'm not sure.

I feel miserable. Probably Craig told Eve and Don about my phone call. I guess they're all laughing at me inside. But I have to get rid of these thoughts or I'll wreck the evening for sure. I tell myself that it's really Derek and Bonita in the backseat and that I have the full power and glory of *Acne* behind me. I am an important person. I'm out on a magazine assignment and here I am, only a sophomore in high school. Nobody else in this car has the backing of a bona fide commercial establishment. I can hardly wait to sign the release.

Five minutes into the evening I know that Eve is after Craig. He is her goal. She should be happy to be with Don, who looks so much like Superman you wouldn't believe it. I'm not a Superman fan, but most girls are. Eve is kind of pretty if you like the glinty, glimmery look. She emits rays; she really does. Not like the sun, but more like what comes from the flashlight of a vigilante. There are tiny hard edges around her face, which is unusual for a high school kid. Some of my friend's faces haven't even formed yet.

"Have you seen *Connective Tremors?*" Craig asks me.

"No."

That's because I didn't want to see *Connective Tremors*. It's a sci-fi thriller that takes place inside somebody's arteries.

"Would you like to see it?"

"Love to."

The theater is only a few blocks from my house, so there isn't much chance to talk. What chance there is gets monopolized by Eve. She talks a blue streak. She's *on,* with no intermissions.

The theater is crowded, but fortunately we don't have to wait in line to get a seat. I don't know what I would have talked about. Craig buys popcorn for both of us, and we settle into our seats. Craig is sitting on one side of me and Don on the other. Eve, of course, is sitting on the other side of Don. Well, here I am sitting between two of the dreamiest guys in school, all brought to me through the courtesy of *Acne Magazine* and my cousin Lisa. I'm really not doing too badly. I wish the world at large could see me. Maybe they will. In print!

The movie is revolting. Squirting blood and sound effects that rip through your head. Sitting in the movies is a great time to look at someone's profile, but it's known to be a great time to do that, so I stay away from that sort of thing. However, just once I look at Craig's on the right of me, and Don's on the left of me. I have a profile too, and it's between theirs, and it's like we're all part of something wondrous like Mount Rushmore. Eve's profile, way over on the other side of Don's, doesn't count.

Craig puts his arm loosely across the back of my seat. I wonder if it's going to descend over my shoulders; but it doesn't. I find that I'm actually getting interested in the movie. It's hard to ignore. One artery is engaged in mortal combat with another artery. At least, that's what it looks like. Horror pictures have so many variations these days that you have to be a genius to know what some of them are supposed to be saying. This picture is supposed to have a psychological as well as a pharmacological message. It's trying to make an antidrugs statement, so help me.

After the movie Craig drives to The Falls, which is a kind of restaurant-bar of medium respectability. It once had a phony waterfall, which caught on fire. The waterfall wasn't replaced, but the name stayed. We have hardly said anything to each other. Just a bunch of artery jokes.

We slide into a booth. Me beside Craig and across from Don. Mount Rushmore broken up.

"Did you like the movie, Shari?" This from Craig, as if he's really acquainted with me.

I try to think of something witty to say.

"It made me see spurting red," says Eve, feeling confident that a more clever answer couldn't possibly exist.

Don and Craig laugh.

The waitress comes for our order. It's discomfort time. Are we having a meal or a snack? I don't want to order first.

"What would you like, Shari?" Craig asks. Shari again. Maybe he's just practicing saying my name, like trying to remember the alphabet or something boring like that.

"What are you having?"

"The biggest hamburger they've got," he says. But he's looking at me strangely.

"I'll take the smallest hamburger and a Coke," I say. I hope he notices that the Coke idea came entirely on my own initiative.

"Make that two Cokes," he says.

I hardly pay any attention to what Eve and Don

order. I am over my hurdle. Eve keeps looking at Craig. It's easy. He's sitting across from her. She's playing up to him. Lots of smiles, gestures, tilting of the head, and agitation of eyelashes. Don is left with me. Mostly I'm stationary. But I crack a smile.

"I've seen you around school," Don says. Does this make me memorable? "You're a sophomore?"

Where did he get his information? I don't ask.

"You hang around with another girl, a monogrammed girl. That is, she wears *L*'s on her clothes."

"You mean Lisa. She's my cousin. And my friend."

"You look like you have a great time together."

"You're very observant."

There is something kind of interesting about Don. If only I went for Superman.

The food comes. It breaks Eve's conversation, and Craig finally turns and talks to me. "How's the smallest hamburger?"

"Delicious. How's the biggie?"

"Fine."

"May I have a bite?" Eve asks Craig, and she's back in business. She had ordered something fried and fishy.

We sit around for about half an hour after we finish eating. Things loosen up, and I even exchange some friendly words with Eve.

Don and Craig split the check down the middle, and we leave. We all get into Craig's car, and I notice that Eve immediately puts her head on Don's shoulder. Craig starts the motor, and we drive off. There are giggles and the sound of movement in the backseat. I wish cars didn't come with backseats. Trouble often starts in the backseat and moves up to the front seat. Maybe I shouldn't call it trouble. But when a couple starts messing around in the back, it's almost a signal for the front seat couple to start up. Of course, if someone's driving, that makes it tough. But not if someone stops the car. In the mouse-ego society I had been traveling in, my dates were happy with a few kisses, some hugs, and that was about it. They were happy to get a date; let's face it. But tonight there is Superman in the backseat and Gorgeous Guy in the front seat. If Craig stops the car, what should I do?

I can't turn around to see what's happening in back. In fact, I don't want to know. I guess Eve likes Don well enough to be making sounds with him, but she might be the type who would with anyone. I wonder if she'd rather be making sounds with Craig. Craig, who does not stop the car.

He is driving Don and Eve home. He reaches Eve's house. Don and Eve disentangle quickly, so I guess not much was going on back there. Eve says a cheerful good night to Craig and me, and Don walks her to the door. They say a few words to each other. Don kisses her good night. I shouldn't be staring. I stare. Then Don comes back into the car.

Craig drives Don home. I say good night to Don in the car. He leans over and kisses my cheek. Very friendly. Then he walks up the steps of his house two at a time.

Now there is just Craig and me.

I wonder if he's going to drive to some remote place, turn on his car radio, and park. I'll be insulted if he does and insulted if he doesn't.

Craig drives me home. But he turns off the motor and makes no move to leave the car. He turns toward me. "Why did you call me up?"

The question sounds abrupt, but it's not said abruptly. There is curiosity in his voice, interest, and I don't know what else. Something big may be hanging on my answer. I can't come out and say I'm *attracted* to him and have been for a year. I can't admit that. And I can't tell him about *Acne Magazine,* because maybe he'll think I don't care about him at all but just find him technically gorgeous.

I reply, "I wanted to meet you."

"Well, that's obvious," he says. "I don't mean that the way it sounds. Do you always call guys you want to meet?"

"Now, just hold on! I think it's okay to call a guy, but I don't make a habit of it. You were my first one."

I'm saying more than I want to say. He knows I like him. If he doesn't know, he's a moron.

Now it's my turn. "I have a question. How come you made a date with me for the very next night?"

"I was free, and I was curious."

Craig's direct answer makes me feel more evasive than ever.

Craig steps out of the car, comes around, and opens my door. We walk up to my front door. He says "I'll call *you* next time," and he looks as if he's going to kiss me. But he doesn't. There must be something about me that changes his mind. I hope it's not my face. Maybe he is trying to solve the puzzle of me.

I say "Thanks" and "Good night," and I open my front door and walk inside. I hear Craig's car drive off. He's gone. Forever?

9

Dad and Gloria Jean are coming for a visit. Mom got a telegram from Dad saying we should expect him and Gloria Jean this week. No particular day. I used to think that telegrams were for something urgent or for happy or sad occasions. But Dad sends them as regular means of communication. Getting a telegram out of the blue can make you uptight, but Mom, Milton, and I are so accustomed to them that it just seems normal. Almost normal.

We never have anything much to do to get ready for these visits. Dad and Gloria Jean stay at the same posh hotel each time, and there's always a casserole at our residence for those who want to eat with us. About the only thing we do to get ready for Dad and Gloria Jean is to get more and more tense.

This time we don't have much of a chance to do that. About an hour after the telegram arrives so do Dad and Gloria Jean. When I hear a car door slam, and then a couple of minutes later hear another slamming car door, I know it's them. What always happens is that first Dad gets out of the car, and then he goes around to open the door for Gloria Jean. Gloria Jean is one of these last-minute rearrangers, and she sits there looking in the car mirror and then looking for things in her pocketbook, and then doing a general reassembling job on herself. So the two-minute interval between the slamming of the car doors tells me that Dad and Gloria Jean have arrived.

Mom is in her Designer Room, and Milton is doing homework in his room. I'm the only one available to open the door, and Dad and Gloria Jean are now coming up the walk.

Whenever I see Gloria Jean with Dad, one of my basic fears is alleviated. I'm afraid that no guy will ever ask me to marry him. I know it's not in style for girls to be afraid of that anymore. And they can always do the asking just like I called up Craig Andrew and asked him to meet me. And there's also the matter of a career, which I'm planning to have. But still I'm afraid I'm going to get left out of being picked for marriage. I'm afraid until I once again see Gloria Jean and know that someone picked *her*. In fact, she was picked twice. I don't know what happened to her first husband. Dead or disgusted, I guess. If she can get picked, I can get picked. I think that's a dumb way for me to look at it. I'm not even mentioning love. And it's cruel of me to think of Gloria Jean that way. I can't stand her, but that doesn't excuse my being cruel.

Another thing I think about when I see Gloria Jean is those TV shows where—*SNAP!*—characters just disappear instantly. I can't help it. I often *snap!* Gloria Jean right out of the scene when she shows up with Dad, and that makes us an original family again. Mom, Dad, Milton, me. And no second wife.

I'm so busy daydreaming that I almost forget to warn Mom that we have visitors coming up the steps.

"Mom!" I yell. "Guess who's here!"

Mom doesn't have to guess. She comes out of her room. She's dressed in one of her own creations. She likes to try her designs out on herself. Today she's all in orange. That sounds yucky, but it works. She has turquoise-colored eyes and dark hair, and she makes a great model for her own clothes.

I open the front door just as the bell rings. Gloria Jean and Dad are standing there. My dad is one of those people who look the same year after year until one year you suddenly see the big change that's been accumulating for a long time. I'm always afraid that the latest visit will reveal the big change. It scares me to have my parents growing older. But Dad looks the same.

I can't say that for Gloria Jean. She has changed herself over. She's recognizable by her trademark, the tea bags, of course, but everything else seems different. She used to be heavy, but now she's slim. So far so good. But what she's taken off in weight, she's put on her face in makeup. Her face is loaded. I take a quick inventory. Eyebrow pencil, eyeliner, mascara, eye shadow, shiner, blusher, powder, lipstick, foundation, white cream, pink cream, and little gold dots have been transferred from their respective containers to her face. She looks like a hooker.

"Hi, honey," Dad says, and he hugs me and gives me a big kiss. By now Milton has come downstairs, so he gets a hug and kiss of equal size. Gloria Jean then leans over and bestows a light kiss on us, depositing in the process some blusher and eyeliner.

Mom sort of shakes hands with Dad and Gloria Jean, and we all sit down in the living room, except Milton, who goes to the kitchen to make instant coffee, and gets what's left over from the cake Gabriel brought the other night.

"You're looking well, Theo," Dad says to Mom.

"So are you, Tom," Mom says.

"Did you redecorate since I was here last? It looks different."

"No," Mom says.

"You're growing," Dad says to me.

"I guess," I say to Dad.

As you can tell, it's a zombie conversation going nowhere. Milton comes in with the food.

"You must come in so handy for your mother!" Gloria Jean exclaims.

As if she's interested in my mother. I wish it took time for me to wind up to get irritated by Gloria Jean. Unfortunately, it usually happens instantly.

"Milton must take after Tom," Gloria Jean goes on. "Tom seems to anticipate my every wish. He's so wonderful to have around."

Gloria Jean has great pride of ownership in my father, which she never fails to convey to my mother. Maybe she does own my father. Maybe she bought him with her first husband's money.

Mom is so used to this bull that she doesn't let it annoy her. Or at least visibly annoy her. As for my father, it seems to go sailing right over his head.

Milton sits down and joins us around the coffee table. We all drink our instant coffee and pick away at the cake, which is now stale. Everyone is silent. We look like a scene from one of those movies where they try to depict tension by showing everyone sitting around a table glumly picking at their food.

Gloria Jean says, "Delicious cake, Theo."

I hate it when she calls Mom Theo, like they're friends or something. Mom is friendlier with the postman, and he calls her Mrs. Stapleton.

Milton knows the cake is lousy. He says, "Mom didn't bake this. She's got a special friend who delivers these cakes."

Dad and Gloria Jean pick up at the words *special friend,* and wait for more. But Milton has said exactly what he wanted to say. No more. No less.

I'm anxious to talk to Dad alone—to be his daughter. I want to tell Gloria Jean to go out and start shopping. She could open her own store and just sell the makeup right off her face if she's tired of being a career shopper. But there's something needy and pathetic about her transformation.

"You've lost some weight," I say, trying to give a compliment.

"Oh, yes, at this most delightful spa." She turns to Mom. "Do you belong to a spa?"

"No."

"Neither do I," says Milton. "Do you have a rash?"

Gloria Jean looks down at her arms. "A rash? Why, no. Where do you see a rash?"

"On your face," Milton says. Milton isn't up on

makeup blushers. He equates too much red on the face with rashes and sunburns.

Gloria Jean is glaring at him. Is he a young innocent or simply bratty?

"Wash your mouth out," she says.

"Shut up, Gloria Jean." This comes from me. *Me.* But I'm not finished. "You've got a rash on your brain."

And there it is. Civilized behavior is just one small step removed from uncivilized behavior. Politeness wears a fragile crown, easy to topple and come tumbling down. That sounds like it's from someone famous, but I made it up on the spot to fit this occasion.

Gloria Jean finally gets her award, presented by me, for years of poor performances. When she first married Dad, there should have been some rules. Gloria Jean should not visit the remains of the family she cut up. If we had had just that one rule, we would not have had five years of hypocritical politeness.

Gloria Jean is now fuming. She turns to Mom. "You should teach your kids some manners!"

What kind? How to break up a family politely?

Mom opens her mouth, but Gloria Jean storms out of the house before Mom can say anything. Dad looks at us, shrugs, and follows Gloria Jean.

Milton starts to laugh. Mom joins him. Then

I'm laughing, too. Mom puts her hands on my shoulders. "You were extremely rude to Gloria Jean," she says. "Congratulations!"

"Do you mean it?"

"Not really. It's just that I can't stand these visits. I don't need any reminders that your father left me. And why. Some divorces can get theorized away as if they're some kind of scholarly dissertation. Just mention psychological problems, sexual problems, compatibility problems, philosophical problems, and everyone nods understandingly because you fall into a kind of academic slot. But I didn't have one of those divorces. It's humiliating to have a divorce you can't justify in big empty words. Your father simply left me for *her*."

"But she's big and empty, Mom. And he really didn't leave you for *her*. He left you for her money. I've got a word for it. Greed. How about that? Dad was greedy."

Mom of course knows this. Dad had a store in town and it did well. But Gloria Jean was in another league. She had real wealth. Dad was dazzled by it.

"But that makes me some kind of commodity your father invested in until he found himself a better deal."

"Oh, come on. You know better. He really loved you. Maybe he still does."

"I don't care anymore." Mom brightens. I know she's going to talk about Gabriel. "You know what's kind of ironic? Gabriel's life is all tied up in figures. Money. He's very practical. In fact, finally last month he stopped charging me for his accounting services. There's not an ounce of poetry in Gabriel. When I first met him, I thought he was about as thrilling as a balance sheet. But now I think he's exciting. He's a solid, good person. And brilliant. You wouldn't believe the tax deductions he came up with. I just hope you and Milton like him."

"You mean like him in a permanent way?"

"Maybe."

"I've liked him that way ever since the night of the plaid jacket."

Mom looked puzzled.

"I can't explain it, Mom. Just believe me that the answer is yes."

10

Lisa is busy writing everything down, and I am busy being honest with her. Every nuance of my date with Craig Andrew gets turned over to her custody. I include the information that Don Berelson has noticed her around school. I know that this won't go into her article, but instead will go into her head, where it will be milked for all it's worth. It will be microscopically analyzed and become the foundation for numerous fantasies. I am glad I was able to bring this about.

Lisa is lying on her bed writing. "Derek will kiss me when he reads this!" she says.

"Let's hope not," I say. Lisa gives me a nasty look. I think she thinks Derek is cute.

"Get me a release for permission to use my name and I'll sign it," I say.

"Are you sure?"

"More than ever. I really feel like a jerk asking Craig Andrew to meet me, but if I can tell myself that I did it as a project, I won't feel like such an idiot."

"You think Craig thinks you're an . . ." Lisa doesn't finish.

"Whatever. Maybe a boy chaser, which I'm not. You know I'm not, Lisa."

"I know," Lisa says. "When I call Derek today, I'll ask him to send the release. And I'll tell him he'll have a finished story in a few days."

"I want to see the story before you give it to him."

"You do?"

"Of course. What if you make me sound stupid?"

"Oh, come on, Shari. But there is one thing. If Craig would just call you, *one* call, that would round out my story. Make it a success story. It needs some kind of windup."

"Why does it? I met a gorgeous guy. That's all I was supposed to do. If other girls want to meet one, let them go to the nearest pay phone. I showed them the way."

"You did great, Shari. Some day, when I'm executive editor at *The New York Times,* there'll be a job for you as an assignments person."

"The *Times*?"

"Well, *Acne* is just the beginning of my rise to

fame and success, which I hope will be meteoric."

"Not if you write complicated sentences like that." I walk toward the door. "I'll leave you alone with your writing."

"Let me know instantly if you hear from Craig," Lisa says in the midst of her scribbling.

"My shouts will be audible," I say.

A few days go by. No phone call from Craig. I try to catch sight of him at school, but when I see him, he doesn't see me. Maybe he sees me when I don't see him. But I wouldn't know that. Anyway, no contact.

A release arrives from D & B Press. Lisa gave Derek my address because he told her he wanted to "deal directly" with me. Here's the deal. The release is a tidy little document, which nevertheless appears to be written on part of a bag from a supermarket. It's brown, and I thought legal papers were white. I also thought they were typed or printed. This one is hand-written. In green ink. It gives *Acne Magazine* and D & B Press permission to use my name without compensation in a forthcoming article titled "How to Meet a Gorgeous Guy." It says I can't seek legal redress for their doing it and I hold them blameless, etc. It also says something about my being fully authorized to enter into this agreement. I know I shouldn't sign anything without showing it to Mom or Gabriel or a lawyer or somebody, but then I'd have to tell them about Derek and Bonita and *Acne*. Also, I'm ninety-nine-percent sure that my signature is worthless because I'm a minor. I'm smarter than they think.

I mail the signed release to Derek, who has enclosed a self-addressed, stamped envelope "for your convenience." Maybe he should have put the stamp money toward another chair.

I now assess where I'm at. Craig hasn't called and won't call. *Acne* is going to be a very unfamous magazine. And so my life is just about back to where it was before Lisa saw the ad.

I'm wrong. One afternoon after school, where incidentally Craig and I saw each other at a distance and he waved and walked on, I'm watching TV. I like the fluffy shows where they interview fluffy people.

I hear the names Derek and Bonita Prissamber. Incredible! But there they are walking with great purpose up to the interview couch while the host beams at them as if they were clean. They look a *little* cleaner than they did in the rat hole, but not much. They sit down and face the cameras. They are wearing shoes.

The host asks them to tell "all of the listening and watching audience out there" about their "super" and "innovative" new teen magazine.

I can't believe this. Derek and Bonita are now *legitimate*. And famous. Everyone who goes on this program seems to land up automatically on other programs and in the press. This show could make the biggest bores in the world famous. In fact, it's doing that right now.

"We're anticorporation, antiplastic, anticliché," Bonita grunts. "We're a right-on, upfront publication. That's why we call ourselves *Acne*."

Milton runs into the room. "Whatcha watching?" he asks.

"Shh," I say.

He looks at the screen. "Jerks," he says, and he runs out.

I've missed a few snatches of conversation. Something about an article written by a teenager about an average teenager wanting to meet a gorgeous guy. "So right in line with what teenagers subliminally, covertly, and psychosocially crave," Derek is saying. "Sure, plenty of kids are cerebral, and we editorially encourage that aspect of them. But we also legitimize and articulate their sensual needs and yearnings."

"Uh, does that mean, if I'm not using too strong a word, you're a racy publication?" The host is clearly hopeful.

"We're essentially a good-taste publication, if that answers your question," says Derek.

Bonita adds, "Our basic thrust is in that direction. We empathize strongly with the average clean-cut teenager."

"Yes," says Derek. "Average is where it's at."

Oh, God! They're getting more and more famous as they sit there. Millions of people are watching. And suddenly it's *my* personal life they're chatting about. My personal life that I've released to the world on a brown piece of paper with green ink.

Derek goes on. "The average teenager wants romance. We call it the cuddle-and-snuggle factor. What *our* magazine is saying, in essence, is that you can have acne and have romance. That's a message that up to this point has been skillfully kept away from teenagers. Teenagers are the most consistently manipulated segment of our population, you know."

The host nods understandingly. "Now for the hard questions," he says. "What qualifications do you have for this enterprise?"

Bonita grunts, "I'm a retired professor of English."

Derek kind of folds his hands across his YOU CAN LIVE WITH ACNE T-shirt and says, "I have a Ph.D. in English from Harvard."

The host beams. See, all of you out there, my program has class.

I'm dying! It's too much! A retired professor and a Ph.D. from Harvard. These flakes are real people. Or maybe just educated flakes. If Lisa is watching, she just fell in love with Derek. Educated guys turn her on, and she already thinks he's cute, acne T-shirt and all.

There's a commercial, and Derek and Bonita are finished. Maybe I am, too. What if Craig's name gets in the magazine? What will he think of me?

The telephone rings. It's Lisa. She watches fluff, too. "Did you see it?" She's gasping. "You'll be more famous than me because you're so average."

"Are they using Craig's name? They can't, can they?"

"Of course not. He's Renaldo."

"Renaldo?"

"Yeah, they picked it to go with Penelope if they used Penelope."

"Well, tell them to use Penelope. I want my name out of that magazine. Out, out! What if it's porno?"

"Oh, be a sport," Lisa says.

"Get my name out," I say, "or I'll sue the acne right off Derek's T-shirt. Now get to work on Penelope. Be firm."

I hang up. I feel bewildered by the way things get connected to one another. How can anything that starts out in a seedy rat hole land up on national TV? Easy. Derek and Bonita are hustlers.

And Lisa identifies with them. She envies them. She wants to emulate them. Lisa doesn't much care whether she becomes a famous and successful writer or a famous and successful rock star or a famous and successful cretin. Just as long as she's famous and successful.

The phone rings. I answer. "Are they using Penelope?"

"Who's Penelope?"

It's Craig.

11

"Want to go for a walk?" It's Craig asking.

We used to have a dog, and when I'd ask her this question, her ears would pick up and her tail would pick up and happiness would spread over her body. You could see it.

I can't see my happiness, but I can feel it. I hate guys who say they're going to get in touch with you and never do. Maybe it's the easy way out to say something like that at the end of a date, and you're not supposed to think it means anything. Sometimes you hope it doesn't. What if you don't want to see the guy again?

I want to see Craig. I want to go for that walk.

"Okay," I say.

"How about now?"

"Now is okay."

"I'll be over in about ten minutes."

"Okay."

We hang up.

I don't have time to think about anything except that it's probably a good policy to wash your hair for incoming as well as outgoing phone calls. But how can you, unless you know they're coming in? Too late now.

I would like to do something constructive while I wait, but I settle for breathing regularly.

The doorbell rings. I open the door. Craig is wearing a thick sweater. I'm wearing a sweater, too.

"Hi," he says.

"Hi."

I go right out with him. It's chilly outside. I think weather is boring, but now with the leaves on the ground and this chill in the air and Craig and me walking side by side, it all adds up to a nice atmosphere. If the wind blew slightly, that might give an extra touch, but the air is still.

Craig starts to talk. "I came by to say I'm sorry. I shouldn't have quizzed you the way I did."

"That's okay. Forget it."

"I'm still curious, I admit that."

Craig seems to be waiting for me to relieve his curiosity.

"Maybe you came by because you're still curious."

I shouldn't say that, but I do.

He doesn't seem to mind.

"I *am* curious, but I'm also sorry. Understand?"

"Yeah."

"I'd ask you to go for something to eat, but I've got to go over to Mom's clinic. I work there Monday and Wednesday afternoons. I like social work. Not that I actually *do* any, but it's neat being around it."

"Are you thinking about going into it?"

"How'd you guess?"

We both laugh.

We start back toward my house. Now there's a little breeze.

Craig says, "Don is planning a party. He's trying to get a bunch of guys together so that it'll be a party that guys are throwing for girls instead of the other way around."

"A guys' party?"

"Yeah. Nothing is definite, but I'm just mentioning it to you."

Strange. Is he inviting me or isn't he? I know that Craig hasn't made up his mind about me. He's put off by the way we met. But it can't be undone. And it can't be explained. But maybe it's the entire basis of any interest he has in me. It makes me fascinating.

We're back at my house. Once again he tells me

that he'll call. This time I know he will. It's broad daylight, so I figure he won't try to kiss me good-bye. I figure right.

I go back into my house.

I am grateful to *Acne* while at the same time I wish it would drop from the face of the earth.

12

Should I apologize to Gloria Jean? Mom says it's up to me. Milton says it's insane. But Dad is caught up in the middle. He and Gloria Jean are still at the hotel. She's buying out New York, and he comes over to our house alone.

I could simply act on principle. But I don't know what the principle is. I was rude to Gloria Jean, but Gloria Jean is worse than rude. If you say something that's rude, you get called down for it, but if you do something that's really terrible and it's spread out over a period of time it's diluted, and then you've got a good chance of getting away with it.

I tell Lisa about the problem. "A rash on the brain!" she screams. "I *love* it. Can I steal it?"

"Anytime. Just don't return it to me. What should I do about Gloria Jean and Dad?"

"You've got a tough one there," Lisa says. "But I'd try to think of it from your Dad's angle. You care about him, don't you?"

"Yes, but I'm disappointed in him."

"I know it," Lisa says. "But be big about it. Your Mom is. Otherwise she wouldn't have let old Tea Bags into the house all these years." Lisa points to the phone. "Why don't you call old Tea Bags right now and say you're sorry. Just do it. What does it cost you? Lies are cheap."

"I'm trying to figure out the principle of this."

"There isn't any principle. What you're doing is called expediency. Want to go home and wash your hair first?"

But Lisa is already looking in the telephone directory. "Here. I've got the hotel number. I'll dial for you."

Lisa dials and then hands me the receiver. "Remember, it's for your father."

"Hello." Dad answers.

"Dad?"

"Well hi, honey. How goes it?"

"Well, I feel really bad about what happened. And so I'm calling to apologize to Gloria Jean for being rude."

"Well, that's *wonderful*," Dad says. He sounds so

good that I silently bless Lisa for giving me the advice to call. For, in fact, doing the dialing.

"I'll get Gloria Jean," Dad says. "She was just on her way out, so hold on." Dad is *so* enthusiastic. I hear him yelling. "Gloria Jean? It's Shari, and she's calling to apologize to you."

I hear some mumbling that I can't make out. I hear the receiver being put down, like on a table, and then picked up again. I hear Gloria Jean's voice over the wire.

"Wash your mouth out!" she says to me, and she hangs up.

Gloria Jean's vocabulary is not extensive.

13

I'm going to be a model. Not the kind you see on magazine covers, who look too good to be true. Although, I'd like to be one of those just once and have hordes of photography experts and lighting experts and makeup experts and prop experts and clothes experts and wet-your-lips-and-say-cheese experts hovering over me just to make *me* look good. But who needs a job where you're washed up at twenty, or is it down to eighteen? Of course, if you look average, you're washed up before you start.

I'm not getting paid, and the only expert around will be Mom, because it's a local fashion show. She won't have much time for me, though. There's a big luncheon on Saturday for some ladies' medical auxiliary, and they're having a fashion show featuring Mom's clothes. Some of the club members volunteered to be models, including Roxanne Black, who has just come down with the flu. Roxanne is my size, or I am Roxanne's size, so I've been drafted to take her place. The dress she was supposed to wear would put you to sleep, but I'm glad to help Mom out. Lisa offered to take my place because, as you can imagine, modeling is one of the fields where Lisa thinks you can become a quick success, and this would be good practice. But Lisa is a little big in the rear. She's really cute and she has a kind of windy midwestern look that comes straight from New York, but still, she's big *there*. Mom is afraid that the dress wouldn't work with Lisa in it.

It's Saturday afternoon and I am in the dressing room of this mansionlike restaurant where the luncheon is being held. It's not a real dressing room but we're using it that way. Me and lots of middle-aged ladies, plus some older and some younger. I don't like to see older women in their underwear. It shows me where I may be someday. Even with their clothes on some of these ladies are nothing to brag about. Nobody pays any attention to me because I'm an underage alien.

When I grow up, I wonder if I'll belong to

clubs. I suppose it's a good idea to do community things and be sociable and social, but I bet it can be a real drag.

Mom is flitting around, trying to help everyone at once. She's the big shot today, but she's working hard. It's a miracle how she got all these outfits ready. To be honest, her miracle is partially composed of four women and two men who are more or less Mom's permanent sewers and help make all her clothes. The club women are just having fun, but shows like this are one of the ways Mom makes a living. She picks up new customers. The ladies are mostly rich because they're married to doctors. I wouldn't want to get rich that way. You think of some poor sick person getting pieces cut out and stitched up and being all bloody and full of tubes, and there you have it, a new car or a vacation in Europe for the doc and his wife.

Mom is passing around programs to remind the ladies about the order of appearance. I look down at my program for a crossed-out name. I find it. Roxanne Black is crossed out. Shari Stapleton is printed in. Then I see a familiar name. Andrew. Sophie Andrew. Craig's mother! What's she doing with all the doctors' wives? I find out later that the medical auxiliary membership is open to any woman who does things to or for the body or mind or is married to anybody who does likewise. They had a big debate about letting in a woman from a borderline massage parlor, but even she made it. Nobody speaks to her, but they accept her dues, as they are always desperate to get money for building new wings onto old wings of hospitals.

So which one is Craig's mother? I look around. Lisa says you can always tell a social worker, but she never specified how. Maybe Mrs. Andrew looks serious. She has a serious profession. So I just have to pick out the one woman who looks like she's not having any fun. I do. It's Mom. Everybody else is full of laughs. I hope Mom gets to eat lunch later. I saw the menu and there's no casserole on it.

The music is starting outside the room, which means the show is about to begin. I look in a mirror. *Everybody* is looking in a mirror. My hair is pulled to one side, and I'm wearing a pair of Mom's high heels. Not bad. I've got good thick hair, kind of wheat-colored, and it usually swings around my face, kind of like a pendulum. But today it's still. My dress has big flowers all over it, and I have a flower in my hair. It all looks better than I thought it would.

We line up in a row according to the order on the program. Now it doesn't take too many brains to know which lady is Sophie Andrew. She's in back of Sylvie Farber and in front of Olive Cook. Olive Cook must be about ninety. They should put her on first just to be sure she makes it. I'm eight ladies behind Olive. I'm in back of someone named Ethel. Maybe they should put me on first to be sure *I'll* make it. I'm not feeling great. This show isn't my bag. I have to strut out there like I'm a big deal just because I'm wearing an expensive outfit that comes from somebody else's talent. And I have to walk a special dumb way. *Gracefully*. I have to make turns. First to the left, then to the right. Mom coached me in a hurry. Since I have a flower theme, I'm supposed to hold my arms out like petals. Float, she says. Ha! Nobody is going to get my theme. They never did when I was a kid in dancing school. Once I was a tractor, and the word *tractor* was printed on my suit. Still, nobody got it. They thought I was a machine from outer space and that Tractor was my outer-space name. This theme stuff is an assault against humanity.

I wish I were first so it would all be over with. Or I wish I were last so everyone would have had it by the time I got out there. By then half the audience may be in the ladies' room sitting it out. I look at Craig's mother. She's smiling and having as much fun as anyone.

The ladies start to move out, one by one. More than ever I wish I had been number one when I see number one come back. She's *through*. Her face is flushed and she's grinning. She got a big round of applause out there. I heard it. There is a narration going on. A man is delivering it. First he gives the name of the lady; then he describes what she's wearing as she walks around; then comes the applause.

After a while it's Craig's mother's turn, and then Olive Cook's. Olive looks very proud. She's married to the most prestigious doctor in town. He's retired, but he was once involved in a major scandal. Everyone knew he was guilty, but he got off, and when it was over, he came out of it more prestigious than ever. That's what can happen in your higher-echelon scandals.

I shouldn't let my mind drift this way, because my name is coming up next. The lady in front of me has gone off to what I now tell myself is the Marie Antoinette scene—waiting for the ax to fall —accompanied by cheers from the crowd. The lady in back of me gives me a little shove. Ethel is just returning, and everyone is awaiting me. I walk out. I see all these uplifted faces around the tables. The announcer booms my name through the mike: "ROXANNE BLACK!!" I smile. I can't see my mother's face because I can't see my mother. I walk along the runway. I do all of my turns and floating correctly. I feel proud, like Olive Cook. It's intoxicating, everybody watching me. For one moment in my life I don't feel average.

My turn is over. The applause starts. I have to go back to the dressing room. I want to do it once more, all over again. I want to be looked at and applauded. But the lady who was in back of me has come out. I wouldn't do it again anyway, and mess up Mom's show.

When I get back into the dressing room, Sophie Andrew comes up to me. Just like that! "You're a friend of Craig's, aren't you?"

"Uh, yes."

"Well, I'm so happy to meet you," she says, extending her hand. "Craig told me he went out with you recently."

"Uh, yes."

What is this? Guys don't deliberately tell their mothers who they go out with. They might grunt the name like Bonita grunts, or they might accidentally spill it or casually mention it. But they don't really tune their *mothers* in to it, and Mrs. Andrew seems tuned in to me. She's a social worker, so maybe Craig tells her *everything*, thinking she has the lowdown on what makes kids tick. And specifically, what made me call Craig in the first place. She'd better not be analyzing me right now.

We're getting jostled and pushed by the women who are now standing around chatting, and changing back into their civilian clothes. This is my chance to escape from scrutiny.

"I have to get out of my flowers before I wilt," I say. Maybe she'll pass the word to Craig that I'm witty. Unless my remark has hidden meaning known only to social workers and she'll pass that hidden meaning on to Craig. Very educated people drive me up the wall because I imagine that their education enables them to ferret out my secrets. But there is nothing in a college curriculum—no textbooks, no field work, no experiments, no frogs, no test tubes—*nothing* that would come close to revealing the existence of *Acne Magazine*.

I tell Mrs. Andrew that it has been very nice meeting her.

14

What really strikes me funny about fame is how fast it can fizzle. Like here today, gone today. After Derek and Bonita showed up on the fluff show, I thought their fame would spread and spread. It would seem invincible because that's how fame is while it lasts. But Derek and Bonita dropped out of public sight. At least, my public sight and Lisa's. We both read newspapers eagerly, watched all the fluff shows, and read the fluff magazines. With all our looking we found just one small item about *Acne* in a magazine far away from the fluff circuit. It was in the latest issue of *Harvard Magazine* under a section called "John Harvard's Journal," which gives news about alumni. Lisa's father gets that magazine because he graduated from Harvard.

Under arts and sciences, and between write-ups

about people who had written books with titles you can hardly pronounce, and who, in addition, are deans, professors, and chairpeople of something or other, there's an item about *Acne Magazine* and Derek Prissamber. If you read it fast, you'd think he was onto something big in dermatology. If you read it slow, same thing.

"This makes me a part of Harvard," Lisa excitedly explains to me. Logic isn't one of her strong points. "Isn't it great that the academic community is behind Derek?"

"*Way* behind," I say. I think that's very funny. Lisa doesn't. "They'll never catch up with Derek," I add.

"Ha ha," says Lisa. "Well, I'm honored to be a part of *Acne*."

"Well, I'm not. How are you coming along with getting my name out and Penelope in?"

Lisa hesitates.

"You *are* getting my name out?"

"I told Derek very strongly and very emphatically that you don't want your name used."

"And what did he say?"

"He said he'll see what he can do."

"That's another way of saying no."

"He means it. It all depends on where the printing's at. See, everything's already at the printer's, but Derek promised me he'd check with the printer and see just what stage he's in. Personally, I think you'll be sorry to be out of it. Look how scholarly *Acne* has become. This will probably be your only chance ever to get into *Harvard Magazine*."

"I'll risk it."

Lisa gets a pair of scissors to cut out the Harvard write-up, and I walk home. It's a day a lot like the one when I took the walk with Craig. Cool and leafy. I try not to think about Craig or about *Acne* being published very soon. All I have to do is wait for time to pass, and then things will fall into place or fall apart.

I wish it were that easy with my family problem. Gloria Jean wants nothing to do with me or Milton. That sounds more like a solution than a problem. But Dad is devastated over it. He has been at our house almost every day while Gloria Jean goes shopping. He has been spilling stuff to Mom about his marriage. It's not good stuff. Mom is sympathetic, but that's it. She makes a point of introducing Gabriel to Dad.

One afternoon Dad comes over while Mom is out. I think he wants to talk to Milton and me alone. He phoned first to see who would be home and who wouldn't. He rang the doorbell when he got here. That always gets me. Ringing a doorbell to get into what was once your own home. But we didn't lock Dad out of his home. He dumped us. I shouldn't say dumped, but that's how I feel sometimes. Like a baby left on a doorstep with a PLEASE TAKE CARE OF HER note and a blanket. Or an unwanted dog deposited at the pound. Or an old person ushered into a bleak cubicle by a white-coated attendant who goes out for a beer and never comes back. Milton says I'm off my rocker to think this way. We have a house and central heating and love and Mom and one another.

Dad does phone us a lot and asks about our report cards, our health, and our hobbies. He sends presents, too. And of course there're his visits with Gloria Jean.

Once Milton had a temperature of 105°, and Dad rushed to town. Milton's temperature dropped the next day. Dad turned around and went back. Since then Milton calls him "Catastrophe Dad."

"See, we haven't been dumped," Milton explained to me. "A dog left at the pound doesn't get this much attention. Maybe the dumper misses him for a couple of days but then remembers all the messes the dog made and how he used to drink from the toilet."

"That's enough, Milton. I get your point."

In some way that *I* couldn't quite manage Milton accepted the divorce. To him Gloria Jean was simply like one of those advertising blimps that hover around your house from time to time, deliver their message, and take off.

Milton, Dad, and I are sitting around the kitchen table. We're each having a sandwich and milk. Suddenly Dad says, "I want to see more of you kids from now on."

"How?" asks Milton.

"I'll come visit. By myself."

"And stay *here*?" I ask.

"No. But I'll be around, and we can do things together."

There's a sadness about him that bothers me. I know I still love him a lot or it wouldn't bother me. His new marriage is a disaster. He got what he wanted, but it was a package deal. He didn't want the whole package. Now he knows it. I think he needs us. That's another thing that bugs me about him. I always have to try to understand him. It should be the other way round. I'm still growing up. He should be wondering how his daughter is turning out. A daughter shouldn't be wondering why her father turned out the way he did.

"Let's plan a definite schedule of visits," he says.

He sounds hopeful. He sounds pathetic. Now Dad's the dog in the pound.

A few days later Dad and Gloria Jean leave. I cry a little.

15

"I have to have a business conference with Derek."

Lisa greets me with this piece of information one afternoon. I have been in her house for two seconds, maybe one.

"About what?"

"All kinds of things. Details. Suggestions. Ideas. Parts of ideas."

"And you want me to come along again?"

"Oh, no!"

I look at Lisa suspiciously.

"Well, I'm not planning to go to his office," she explains. "And anyway, why should I bother you?"

I'm still looking at Lisa suspiciously. "You want to have a business conference with Derek alone and not in his office?"

"Yeah."

"Otherwise known as Lisa wants to *re*meet a

gorgeous guy. This is just a plan for you to see Derek again, isn't it?"

"You admit that Derek is gorgeous?"

"Well, I was just—"

"Forget it. He's intellectually gorgeous. You can't see it if you're not on the same beam. Anyway, Derek needs me."

"What?"

"Guys with holes in their clothes and peeling walls and a grunting mother need a girl."

"Really?"

"It's a fact." Lisa sighs. "Maybe a business conference isn't such a hot idea. He'll just think of me as business. I need to do something a little different."

"Okay. Play hard to get. Stay away from Derek forever."

"Cut it out, Shari. I *really* like him."

I believe her. And I don't want to hurt her feelings. "It's just that Derek's a little weird, Lisa. Not like the guys at school."

"Exactly! That's the point. He's sophisticated. Now you understand, and you can help me. I definitely don't want to go to his office. It's so businesslike there."

Businesslike? How would she describe the county dump?

Lisa goes on. "I want to meet with him somewhere else. Out of doors, perhaps. Someplace romantic."

"Lisa, it's chilly out there."

She isn't listening. "And I'll need a new dress that'll go with the atmosphere."

"Lisa, I think you should stay indoors. And try to do something kind of grown-up. Derek is an adult."

"That's what I've been telling you. So what's grown-up?"

"Invite him for lunch. Lunch is very big with adults. They're always having lunch with one another."

"But where would we eat?"

"Right here at your house."

"What about my parents?"

"Ask them to go out for a while. Tell them you're having a Harvard graduate for lunch. Your Dad will like that."

"But Dad will want to meet him. Wait. Never mind. My parents are going to an auction Saturday. I could do it then. One problem. I don't know how to cook. What'll I serve Derek?"

"No problem. I'm sure I can let you have a casserole."

Lisa goes straight to the telephone and dials Derek's number, which I guess she knows by heart.

"Derek? Hi. Oh, you recognized my voice. So,

how've you been? Oh, no, I'm not calling about the article. This is a social call. Can you come to lunch this Saturday?"

There's a long pause.

"What do you mean, *why*? Well, let me put it this way. I'm not just a cool, efficient business person. Underneath it all I'm, well, I'm a pastoral type. But I'm inviting you for an indoor lunch because it's chilly outside."

Lisa is looking at me as if she wants me to reconfirm that. I nod. I'm remembering my phone call to Craig, with Lisa standing by. Now our roles are reversed.

Lisa's call is working. She is saying "noon," and she's giving Derek directions to her house. After she says good-bye she's ecstatic. "He's coming! He's coming!"

I'm happy for Lisa, even though the prospect of Derek coming to my house would cause me to bolt all the doors.

On Saturday I deliver the casserole. I'm amazed at Lisa's efficiency. She sprinkles bits of parsley all over the casserole so that it almost looks palatable. She is thawing a chocolate layer cake for dessert, which she got from the frozen section of the supermarket. She has set the dining room table for two, with a bunch of what she calls "bucolic" flowers as the centerpiece. And she is wearing a new dress. Unfortunately, this part of her plan is a real clinker. The dress is about three sizes too tight, especially in the rear, and appears to be shrinking even as Lisa walks around in it. I know she *thinks* she looks sexy, but the dress looks like the victim of a washing machine gone berserk. Maybe I should tell her. But it's almost noon. I have to leave her house before Derek arrives.

I hear a sound outside. "He's here!" Lisa whispers.

"I'll go out the back. Have a wonderful time!" I decide not to hug Lisa or even touch her. Her dress might not survive.

I rush to the back of her house and open the door. I hear Lisa opening the front door. I hear her say hello and Derek say hello, and then another voice grunts hello. It's Bonita! Derek has brought his mother.

Poor Lisa. Should I leave or should I stay? Maybe she needs help.

"Oh, Shari!" Lisa is calling me. She needs me.

I walk to the front hall. Derek and Bonita are standing there. They look exactly as I remember them in their office and on TV. Maybe their clothes haven't left their bodies since we first met.

Lisa is sort of signaling me with her eyes. I think

my job is to get rid of Bonita. I turn to Bonita. "Would you like a tour of the neighborhood? We have lots of interesting old trees."

"I'm not into trees."

"Uh, could you help me in the kitchen?"

"I'm not into kitchens."

"Does that mean you don't go into them?"

Suddenly Bonita walks into the living room, sits down on the sofa, and grunts, "I'm a guest."

Derek sits down beside Bonita. "Mom and I simply don't identify with kitchens," he says.

"Well, neither do *I*," Lisa says as we all sit down. "After I graduate from high school I'm going to bypass kitchens completely and go straight to Harvard like my father."

Lisa is waiting for Derek to react to what she has just said. If she drags out her father's Harvard yearbook, Harvard mug, Harvard chair, or Harvard warm-up suit, I'll die. If she says one more sentence like that, I'll die. If I stay here much longer, I'll die. Lisa is like someone who has lost her identity to invaders from outer space in one unguarded moment and become one of *them*. I could be next.

Derek turns to me. "How are things in the world of average?"

I'm safe. Invaders from outer space are looking for superior specimens, not average me.

Lisa interrupts. "This is social, not business, remember?"

"Of course, I remember," Derek says. "That's a very lovely dress you're wearing, Lisa."

Lisa beams. Derek has noticed how she looks. Derek is paying attention to her as a girl. This is what the afternoon project was supposed to be all about. At last it's going well.

Bonita grunts: "Hot water use is one of our national excesses."

"What?" asks Lisa.

"Hot water use," Bonita repeats. "That's a cold-water dress you're wearing, and you used hot water on it. Hot water devastates clothes."

Lisa is speechless.

Derek says, "Water conservation, both hot and cold, is one of the solid basics of Mom's and my existence. We practice it regularly."

"Yes," grunts Bonita. "Abstinence! Abstinence in itself is cleansing. We feel a moral obligation to use as little water as possible."

This I believe. Now I'm pretty sure their clothes haven't been washed since the first time I saw them. I don't even want to think about their bodies.

Lisa is not ready to give up. "I believe in water, too," she says. "That is, water conservation."

"Superb," says Derek. "Then you're probably not one of the thousands of teenagers who overwash their hair. We may devote an article to that phenomenon alone."

"Don't forget the split ends angle," Lisa says helpfully.

"Split ends!" grunts Bonita. "A hair strand is composed of dead cells. How much can you expect from it?"

"Not a whole lot, I guess," Lisa says.

Derek leans toward Lisa. "You might have a great angle there, sweetie. You see, split ends are a kind of teenage tragicomedy. It's a subject we could treat with absolute respect but at the same time place within the context of the entire spectrum of universal mishaps."

"Definitely," Lisa says.

I have to leave. I *have* to leave. Lisa is one of them now. I can't help her. I can only help myself.

I look down at my watch. "Oh, I have to run. Wonderful to have seen you. Bye, everybody." I say these things while rising from my chair, walking to the front door, opening it, and closing it behind me. No one has had a chance to say or do anything. I hope Lisa is still my friend.

I go home. I listen to records and do some homework. It makes me feel normal. Around three o'clock the telephone rings. I answer it.

"It's me," Lisa says. "He loved my dress. Did you notice?"

16

The first issue of *Acne Magazine* is now published and available to the public. What public I'm not sure. I don't see it in the stores, and Lisa and I have gone to at least ten. "I guess there are a few kinks in their distribution system," Lisa says. "And they'll all be ironed out in time for the second issue."

Now we're sitting in her bedroom. We are each clutching a copy of *Acne*. We have been sent twenty complimentary copies in total. Ten for her, ten for me. I sincerely hope that this is the entire pressrun. If Craig Andrew sees this, I will quickly and efficiently kill myself.

First I have to admit that the magazine isn't bad. It isn't sexy or tacky, and except for its name it's better than most of the other teenage magazines

I've seen. But there's the little matter of the article entitled "How to Meet a Gorgeous Guy." I scan it fast. Lisa's name, first, middle and last, is printed in big letters under the title. In smaller letters, but repeated over and over is *my* name. Derek had told Lisa that it was too late to change me to "Penelope." Craig is "Renaldo." Derek hadn't let Lisa see the finished article after he made his "editorial" changes, additions, and deletions. And he said that my seeing it was an absolute "no-no" because I would have fixed it up to make myself seem great. Forget great, I would have fixed it up to make myself anonymous. I start to read the article.

How to Meet a Gorgeous Guy

BY LISA JACQUELINE BLAKELY

Shari Stapleton is a sophomore in a high school in a suburb of New York City. Shari considers herself to be average. A lot of teenagers are average, although it's sometimes hard for them to admit it. I'm, of course, not talking about the superjocks, the cheerleaders, the class wits, the superachievers. If you're not in the above categories or an associated category, it can be tough. Acne Magazine wanted to find out how tough. How tough, for example, is it for the average girl to meet a really gorgeous guy? This article is not for cheerleaders or superachievers. It's for those of you who identify with average. Come along and see how one average girl did meet a gorgeous guy.

Shari Stapleton believes in the telephone. This is the vehicle she uses to meet gorgeous guys. To be more specific, Shari believes in calling from a pay phone. Why? Well, Why *strikes at the very heart of what this article is about. You have to do what's comfortable for you. Also you may have to call a bunch of guys before you find one who is willing to meet you. Be prepared for that.*

First Shari washes her hair to give herself courage. Then she calls gorgeous guy Renaldo. It takes plenty of guts to dial. . . .

I can't read on. "Lisa! This is for the birds! It makes it seem like I called lots of guys."

"Well, Derek just wanted to give the idea that a girl might have to make a bunch of calls before she got to meet a guy. What if an average girl out there tries once and it doesn't work. What if she strikes out a few times? She'll be completely zonked."

I read on. And on. There is no mention of Don and Eve. In fact, there is no mention that "Renaldo" and I went out with another couple.

Most of the facts have been rearranged or obliterated. "Where's Don? Where's Eve?" I ask.

"Derek felt that having another couple waters down the concept," Lisa says. "I wrote up just what you told me. But Derek edited it. I've been learning about the magazine business. Editors have the last word. If they say something's in, it's in. If they say it's out, it's out. They fix up what you write to make it look better. And they take out what they might get sued for. Like if Craig recognized himself."

"I'm stupefied! Derek changed hamburgers to steak dinners. When's the last time any kids you know went out for a steak dinner except with their parents?"

"Steaks have more pow than hamburgers," Lisa says. "What I mean, as Derek explained it to me, is that any guy who'd take you out and pay for a steak dinner must have fallen hard. That means a happy ending. Happier than hamburgers."

Lisa looks depressed. "Gee, Shari, I was hoping you'd like it. I didn't know for sure what would be in the article, but isn't the idea of it, the idea of being in this new magazine, more important than what the article says?"

"No."

"Okay. You're entitled to your opinion. But I think everything's super. I'm . . . well, I'm kind of famous, aren't I? My name's in print in this magazine that will be famous just as soon as they get their distribution problems fixed."

I don't want to deflate Lisa. I don't want to tell her that she has gone from obscurity to near-obscurity. That a magazine with a name like *Acne* will probably sell five copies, all to Derek and Bonita's relatives, although they are the kind of people most relatives probably wouldn't want to acknowledge.

Then I look down on the bed, and it fully dawns on me that Lisa is the owner of ten copies of *Acne*, that she could show them all around school. That Craig Andrew could see them. I try to keep my voice steady as I ask her the next question. "What are you going to do with your ten copies?"

"Pack them away carefully."

"You mean, you're not going to show them to anyone?"

"No one."

"I don't believe you."

"That's a crummy thing to say, Shari."

"I'm sorry. But if you're so hung up on being famous, how can you just pack away these copies without showing them to anyone?"

"Because going around showing the magazine to everyone would be very small-time. *Acne* is national. I'm national. People will see the magazine.

They'll come to *me* and tell me they saw what I wrote."

"What if they don't?"

"They will. See, Derek is seriously thinking of having a teenager permanently on the magazine staff, and he says that if he does it, it will be me. I'd get to do a column every month. So, Shari, if the kids miss this month's issue, there'll always be next month's and the month after. *Acne*'s reputation will grow, and so will mine."

"Uh, did you get paid yet?"

"You're a suspicious soul. I'm getting the whole two hundred bucks, and Derek says to expect my check at the end of the week. I'm splitting it with you."

"Me?"

"Sure. Without your being average I wouldn't have been able to write the article. And you worked hard. The phone call and date and all. I asked Derek to pay you, but he said they're on a tight budget."

"I believe it."

"No cracks." Lisa stacks her ten copies neatly. Then she says, "So, how are things with Craig?"

"I'm waiting to hear from him. I haven't seen him, at least up close, since our walk. I guess he's trying to figure me out."

"Well, wouldn't you if you were in his shoes?"

"Don't be so wise, Lisa. You make me feel inferior."

"That doesn't follow. You're the one who said he's trying to figure you out. I just agreed. Besides, you should never feel inferior. Just average. You keep forgetting."

17

We are invited to Gabriel's mother's house for dinner. This means all of us. Mom, Milton, and me. We've never met Gabriel's mother, but Gabriel must have told her everything about us. I think we are going to be inspected.

Milton is raising a fuss. "Gabriel is too old to be living with his mother. And if he weren't living with her, we wouldn't have to meet her. So I'm not going."

Since Milton is willing to be the family slave from time to time, I think we should give in to him when he wants something—like staying home. But Mom insists.

"You don't want to offend Gabriel's mother, do you?"

"I don't know Gabriel's mother."

"You like Gabriel, don't you?" Mom asks.

"Sure. He's great. Sometimes he talks with too many numbers, but he's great."

"So don't you want to meet this great person's mother?"

"No."

"Is your *no* negotiable?"

"Everything's negotiable."

"You wanted an advance in your allowance so you could see *Connective Tremors*. All right, you've got it if you go with us to meet Gabriel's mother."

"Not worth it."

I butt in. "It's a marvelous movie."

I'm trying to help Mom.

Milton looks at me. "I heard it stunk."

"So, why do you want to see it?" I ask.

"I don't believe everything I hear."

Mom is getting exasperated. This conversation is taking place five minutes before Gabriel is supposed to pick us up to go over to his mother's house. We are all dressed up, including Milton.

"Very well," says Mom. "You can stay home. Just heat up the casserole I left in the freezer."

That does it. It's all so simple when you know the right word. Casserole.

Milton is going to Gabriel's mother's house.

I wish I could be as honest as Milton. I don't

want to go either. I want to stay home in case Craig calls me. This is new with me. Keeping the phone covered at all times is a plan that distinguishes desperate people from normal people. Normal people believe that if somebody really wants to get in touch with them, they'll try again if there's no answer the first time. Desperate people don't take chances like that. They make sure their phone is always answered.

Mom is usually home, and Milton almost always comes straight home after school. And I've discontinued my stops at Lisa's house so I can be home more of the time. But tonight we are all going out and leaving our telephone alone without a sitter. What if Craig calls?

Gabriel picks us up. He looks sharp. He and Mom exchange long looks. She looks sharp, too.

We pile into Gabriel's car and ride to his house. Gabriel is whistling. If his mother were vicious or something, he probably wouldn't be whistling. So the evening is looking up.

We arrive in front of his house. Gabriel and his mother live on the first floor of an old two-family house, which Gabriel owns and which has tax advantages. Gabriel didn't say that, but when you know Gabriel, you know that's the way it has to be.

I guess his mother hears us, because she meets us

at the door. I'm thinking that whatever she's like, this is it for Mom. This is the lady Mom will inherit as a mother-in-law if she marries Gabriel.

Gabriel's mother envelops Mom, Milton, and me before I can get a good look at her. But I already know she's an enveloper. Plump, warm arms, mushy-soft body; she's the opposite of precise Gabriel. And she's so instantly nice that you almost don't believe it.

"I'm so happy to meet all of you," she says. Then she stands back, and I can see her. She has wavy white hair and a kind of plain, eternal-looking face. You can imagine her mother and her grandmother and her great-grandmother all having the same face. And also the same plain dress she's wearing. It's something that Mom, the Dress Designer, would never design, but it's just right for Gabriel's mother. Everything about her reminds you of old-fashioned dependability. Buildings could be torn down around her, neighborhoods demolished, skyscrapers and modern shopping malls erected, everything changing, but she personally remains the same.

You get a warm feeling that this woman will take care of you. That she has a lineup of home-baked custards, ointments, brews, splints, bandages, chicken soup, quilts, hot tea, herbal remedies, corn pads, bed jackets, squashy pillows, and recipes handed down from generation to generation that will fix whatever might be wrong with you. Gabriel has a cushy deal.

Milton is falling under her spell. And when we walk inside and he gets a load of the table she's set in the dining room, he's practically in love. If Gabriel moves out, Milton will move in. The table is banquet-size. There are about three or four different main courses to choose from. Fish, poultry, meat, and combination dishes. There are salads, and soups, and vegetable plates, and relish plates, and rolls, and long loaves of bread, and short loaves of bread, and potatoes, and rice, and food that I never even knew existed. This is a new world. The desserts aren't set out yet. I say desserts, because I know they must be plural.

Gabriel's mother invites us to sit down in the living room, where she offers us drinks. We all say no, thank you. I don't know why Mom said no, but Milton and I are too greedy to stop and drink. We're thinking of what we saw in the dining room.

"Not even a small glass of ginger ale?" Gabriel's mother is speaking to Milton.

"Well, okay," says Milton.

Mom and I and Gabriel have ginger ale too, so Milton won't feel alone. We also have crackers with cheeses. And crackers with chopped liver, which Milton eats because he doesn't recognize the liver. Gabriel's mother brings in more stuff to go with the ginger ale.

This is the setup:

In front of Milton she places peanuts and whole pieces of fruit and sliced-up pieces of fruit and some hot, cute-looking rolled things. Milton gets busy with three honeydew slices, peanuts, and a bunch of the rolled things. I'm now next to some chips, which I demolish, plus various cheeses, cold cuts, and stuffed pickles, all of which I try one at a time. Mom is stationed beside some sour cream dips, Melba toast, and steaming little pancakes with diced-up green stuff on top of them.

We're surrounded.

Gabriel isn't any slouch either. He's making inroads into some tiny pot pies with flaky crusts and something that looks like meringue on top.

Mom looks up from her food to admire a painting on the wall. She gets up to look at it. So Milton and I politely get up too and admire the painting. When we all go back to our seats, we each take a different one than before. Now Milton has the sour cream dips, Melba toast, and steaming little pancakes with the diced-up green stuff. I'm on the peanuts, fruit, and rolled things, and Mom is now working on cheeses, cold cuts, and pickles. Gabriel is content with his tiny pot pies.

My stomach is feeling pampered, and I'm enjoying myself except for the sound I hear. It's the sound of the telephone ringing in my house. My house is miles away from this one, and yet the sound of my ringing telephone is loud and clear. Craig is calling me and he is frustrated because he can't reach me. "To heck with it," he says to himself. He slams down the receiver. "I'll call somebody who's available, somebody who stays by her phone because she has faith that I'm going to call."

Gabriel's mother gives us seconds and thirds of ginger ale. We need them to wash down the food. Then I notice something. She's not eating a thing. She must get her kicks out of presiding over food. She's beaming at us. She sits empty-mouthed in her chair and tells us to call her Bertha.

"Do you cook all the time, Bertha?" Milton asks.

"Every day," Bertha says.

"This is good stuff," Milton says.

"Why, thank you," Bertha says. Then Bertha turns to Mom. "So, you design clothes."

Now we're down to business. Mom is getting sized up.

"Yes," says Mom.

"I guess you never design for anyone as big as me."

Mom is not getting sized up. Bertha is sizing herself up.

Mom says, "I design for all sizes."

Mom is tactful.

"What do you think would look good on me?"

Wthout blinking an eyelash Mom says, "Light blue. And a soft fabric, with long sleeves, a V neckline, and small ruffles around the neck."

Bertha is beaming in a shy kind of way. She looks down at her plain dress. Then she says, "It sounds like you've just about whipped up the dress already."

"It wouldn't be any trouble to make it," Mom says.

Bertha keeps beaming.

"It would be a pleasure," Mom adds.

Something very terrific is happening in this room. Mom and Bertha are hitting it off. They like each other. Milton likes the food and Bertha. So do I. Gabriel is making calculations, and he is coming to the same conclusion as I am. We are a kind of family.

By the time we get up to sit down for dinner, dinner doesn't look all that good. It looks revolting. We're all stuffed except Bertha. She insists that we try everything. She's the type who gets mortally wounded if you don't eat her food. I don't know how Gabriel escaped becoming a fat man. But now I know why he comes over for Mom's dinky old casseroles.

We sit around the table, slowly getting sick. If

Mom marries Gabriel, I see years of gluttony stretching out before me. I wonder if I'll get up from this table a fat person. I wonder if I'll get up from this table. If somebody calls you on the phone, can they tell if you're fat by the sound of your voice?

18

Derek and Bonita have vanished without a trace. It's hard to tell if people like Derek and Bonita have actually vanished because their unoccupied office looks about the same as their occupied office. They left their stuffed chair and the telephone. They also left two dead plants. I feel bad about the plants.

And I feel terrible about Lisa. Her future career is shot. As well as her past career, in a way. Derek and Bonita bolted without paying her. The first thing you think about when people bolt is how many debts they left behind. I learned this from Gabriel the accountant. Derek and Bonita left more than a quarter of a million dollars worth of debts. As far as I'm concerned, this is by far the most impressive thing they did. It sure beats being on the TV show or getting mentioned in *Harvard Magazine*. I think it beats graduating from Harvard. I figure you have to be smarter to get away owing that much money than you do to graduate from Harvard.

"Con artists," Lisa grumbles. She's furious. We are sitting on a train returning from New York City. We have just visited the premises formerly occupied by Derek and Bonita. We have met the owner of the building. Derek and Bonita owe him thousands of dollars in back rent, which is figured into the total. How a person could be taken for that much is beyond me. The owner of the building is a businessman who said he'd been cheated over and over by slick men in three-piece suits. Poor guy. He was ripe for an acne T-shirt to show up and rip him off.

Lisa, of course, was cheated out of a mere two hundred dollars. When the money didn't arrive at the end of the week, she tried to telephone Derek. But his phone had been disconnected. Lisa did not find this encouraging. So today, the day after finding out about the disconnected phone, we checked out the premises, the *ex*premises, of Derek and Bonita. The landlord is the one who gave us the information about Derek and Bonita's huge debt.

Lisa sighs every few minutes on the trip home. "I'll just have to forget about it," she says.

"What else can you do?"

"Well, we've got copies of the one and only issue of *Acne Magazine* ever printed. I guess that's like owning a worthless stock certificate."

"Probably."

"No, it's not," Lisa says, contradicting herself. "*Acne* was nationally published, don't forget."

"So are some worthless stock certificates."

Lisa sighs again. "Those robbers! Those creeps! Those rip-off artists!"

I feel helpless. Derek and Bonita left behind two dead plants and one damaged ego. Lisa's. Her ego is all tied up in *Acne Magazine,* and I think that's scary.

19

I am badly in need of a social worker. Here are my credentials. My parents are split up. I have a wicked stepmother. I have a current crisis brought on by my rash remark. I have guilt feelings. I may be experiencing trauma.

I have a particular social worker in mind. She could be very busy, in which case I'll settle for seeing her son, who works with her on Monday and Wednesday afternoons.

I am, of course, out of my skull to even consider going to Mrs. Andrew's clinic. How else can I run into Craig? I see him at school, but always at a distance. And, I'm not sure about this, but I think for the past few days he's been turning his head away when he sees me. He doesn't acknowledge me. What really freaks me out is that I heard Don is going ahead with that party, the one Craig just about invited me to. Since the party is definitely on, why hasn't Craig contacted me?

My most recent basic strategy about my life was just to remain in limbo until something happened. Well, something happened. A party I am or am not invited to materialized. Maybe Craig will call up the night before the party to tell me what time he'll be picking me up. Maybe that's the way he operates. He assumes we're all set to go to the party together, so it's just a matter of last-minute details. I must be hallucinating if I believe this. I *have* to find out where I stand.

So what's left but to visit my friendly neighborhood social worker who doesn't happen to be anywhere near my neighborhood? Craig's mother operates out of an office downtown. I know where it is because I've known kids who have gone there with their problems or what their parents think are problems or what their teachers think are problems. Going downtown is no big deal for me, but that's when I'm going downtown to the dentist or to shop or to do something I'd ordinarily do downtown.

I think about bringing Lisa in on this. It would help to have someone helping me. But I feel so incredibly *dumb* about what I'm doing. I go alone.

Everyone appears to be doing something normal

downtown except me. Could any of these people passing by on the street be up to anything as nutsy as what I'm up to? It would be comforting if some of them are. I come to Mrs. Andrew's clinic. It's on the ground floor of one of those nondescript buildings that's not particularly attractive and not particularly unattractive. I open the door and walk right into the reception room.

I'm all alert to see Craig. But he isn't there. He's probably in a back room with his mother. I wish I had asked him exactly what he does to help his mother. His mother's consultations are private. He can't sit in on them. No teenager is going to blab off about a problem in front of another teenager unless they're pals. And not in a social worker's office, for sure.

There is a male receptionist sitting behind a desk. I wonder if this has sociological significance. Fortunately he doesn't look up when I come in. He's busy talking with some kids who are standing around the desk. I don't recognize any of the kids. There are about ten people in the reception area, combinations of kids and parents or kids alone. It's very crowded. A few of the kids are sitting on the floor. Mrs. Andrew needs bigger quarters. Some of the kids move away from the reception desk, and the receptionist looks up. At me. Now I'm faced with going through with the whole thing.

I see there's a pile of forms on his desk. That's all I need. A form to fill out. I have a thing about forms. I detest them. I already feel that I've filled out my life's quota of them. Forms are strictly factual, and for every rigid category listed there's implied for me the automatic wiping out of all those qualities *not* listed, the ones on which my feelings as a sensitive and unclassifiable and breathing human being are based. I turn around and walk out of the reception room.

I feel as if I've made an escape. A clean escape. I accomplished nothing, but I lost nothing. I walk along the street, a free person. I'm about three doorways away from the clinic when I see Craig coming toward me! I wonder if he saw me walk out of the clinic. I feel so tense I could fall apart. He is carrying a large white paper bag and some of the white looks greasy. My guess is that he has hamburgers and French fries in the bag. There is a fast-food place just up the street. So this is how he helps his mother. Well, a person has to eat.

Craig sees me. He keeps walking toward me. He gives me a hard, cold stare and keeps walking on, right past me. Right on past.

20

"Do you know Eve Raines?"

We're sitting around the supper table eating our spinach casserole when my mother asks me this question.

"In a way," I answer. "Let's say I know her more than I want to know her. Why?"

"She's coming over tomorrow after school. Wants me to design a dress for her for a party. Odd . . . I usually don't get high school kids. I'm too expensive and too . . ."

"Mature," I say. I shouldn't say that. Mom calls her stuff young and vibrant. "Do you know her mother? I mean, I don't get it. Why she thought of you."

"I don't get it either," Mom says. "I don't know her mother."

"Try to design her something ghastly, will you?"

Mom smiles. "I'll do my best."

I wonder if I should hang around when Eve comes over or stay out of sight. I'm not going to plan either way. If I see her, I see her. If I don't, I don't. I wish I weren't so curious, though.

I'm home when the doorbell rings the next day. Mom answers it. She says hello to Eve, and Eve says hello to her, and Eve walks in. Eve sees me.

"Shari! You live here?" Eve slaps her face lightly. "Of course. You're the Shari of SHARIs."

All at once I know that I'm the reason Eve has come to my house. I hope she doesn't plan a career in acting, because she'll starve. Girls who look like Eve sometimes hope to be actresses. They figure they're halfway there with their looks. But before they get too hopeful they should learn to slap their faces convincingly.

But right now I'm thinking about Mom. Is Eve going to waste Mom's time? Mom's time is worth money.

Eve is full of chatter. "It was such fun getting together with Don and Craig, wasn't it?" she says to me, ignoring Mom.

"Yeah."

"I didn't know that you knew Craig. It was such a surprise when he told Don and me who his date was. Don and I were going out alone, and then

Craig said he had a date, and it was you. Rather last-minute, wasn't it?"

"I guess."

"Well, it's such a coincidence coming here and finding you, because I need this dress for a party I'm going to with Craig, and it's at Don's house."

Three cheers for sublety. No, make that sadism. And three more cheers for the knockout punch. Because that's what Eve thinks she's delivering. She's right. I'm shocked. And I'm sad. Oh, so sad. Craig is taking *her* to Don's party. I wonder what makes kids like Eve the way they are. She could have come up to me at school and told me about the party. She could have delivered the blow there. But no. Sadistic is better. Have Shari's mother make the dress Eve is wearing to the party with Craig. It was too late to wish that Mom had gone into business as the town's first female undertaker.

Mom is looking at me. She knows I went out with someone named Craig, but that's about it. Now the situation is dawning on her. Eve is dawning on her. But Mom smiles sweetly at Eve. I know Mom's smiles. This is going to be fun. Maybe Mom will stick a few pins into Eve during the fitting.

They go into the Designer Room. I hear a shriek. "Eight hundred dollars?" Eve is shrieking.

I hear Mom say, "For the skirt alone, dear." Mom *never* calls anyone dear.

Eve says, "It's a rip-off."

The door opens. Mom is still smiling sweetly. "Eve," she says, "for a thousand dollars I could make your figure look perfect."

"My figure already looks perfect."

She's wrong there. She's skinny.

"Think about it," my mother says as she walks Eve to the door. "But not too long. I get booked way in advance, dear."

"Craig will like me in anything I wear!" Eve says as she walks out. Parting shot.

The door closes behind Eve. "Boy, she's something else," Mom says. "She's a classic trouble-maker."

"But she's going out with Craig Andrew. I went out with him once. Make that once and a half if a walk counts. He hinted that he was going to take me to Don's party. But now he's switched to Eve."

Mom looks like she's ready to drop everything she had planned to do and have a long, comforting talk with me. I'm tempted to let it happen. But Mom can't explain Craig's hard, cold stare. She can offer theories. She can offer sympathy. But she can't produce the reason.

I say, "I have to do my homework."

Mom goes back to her work, and I sit down at the kitchen table with my books. The telephone rings. I pick up the receiver. "Hello."

"Shari? Hi. This is Don Berelson. Remember me?"

Don Berelson is calling me!

I'm happy again. Mom often says that teenagers are "mercurial." Up, down, up. All in an instant.

I'm happy, all right. In the few seconds that it takes Don to say "Shari? Hi. This is Don Berelson. Remember me?" I work out my immediate future. I know that Don is calling to invite me to his party. That quick kiss he gave me on the cheek when he left the car that night actually hid a ton of feelings. I see the way Fate has planned Project Acne to work out for me. I'm supposed to meet a gorgeous guy. I do. It's Don Berelson. Superman. He likes me even though I'm dead-center average. All along the way it has been intended for me, Shari Stapleton, to be happy, to be loved, to be wanted. Because basically life is fair.

"I was wondering if you could give me your cousin Lisa's phone number."

Then again, it's not healthy to think that life is fair, because then you are totally unprepared for its unfairness, which is rampant, epidemic, and a few other descriptions I picked up from Lisa's Harvard-educated father.

"I hope you don't think I'm coming on too fast, but I've wanted to meet your cousin for a long time. I've seen her around, but I don't know anyone who knows her. At least, I didn't. Then I lucked out and met you."

"Lucked out," I repeat listlessly. "You want her phone number? That's what you said?"

"Sure. If you think she wouldn't mind. I'm having a party and I'd like to invite her. Does she like parties?"

"Who doesn't?"

21

I have been dropped by Craig Andrew. I knew it when I got the hard, cold stare on the street. I knew it when Eve Raines told me he was taking her to the party. And I've known it for some time, because it couldn't be just by chance that he turns the other way when he sees me at school. I think back to our walk when he told me about Don's party. He practically invited me to it. But now he's invited Eve. I think about rejection. There are so many ways to get rejected that you can never run out of them. So far, I've collected a cold stare, an invitation turned noninvitation, a face turned the other way numerous times, and telephone calls never made.

Tonight I expect to add to my collection when I go to Don's party. It's stupid for me to go to the party, but I'm going. Jay invited me. He's one of my mouse-ego friends. I didn't want to accept, but I couldn't turn him down. It would be like passing rejection on. When you know how it feels, you don't want to do it to somebody else.

Mom made me a dress to wear to the party. It's the first dress she's made for me in years. Maybe it has some weird kind of psychological connection with Eve coming over to ask Mom to make her a dress for the party. But that doesn't make any sense at all. Whatever it is, Mom and I are both caught up in it, and I've been standing patiently for my fittings.

I am ready for Jay when he arrives to take me to the party. In fact, I'd been waiting for him, because he was late. But I knew he'd come. Guys like Jay always do. When he arrives, he is all dressed up, and there is something pathetic about that because he did it to impress me. I imagine that Jay polished his shoes an extra time and combed his hair an extra time and that's why he's late. We leave for the party right away. Jay is all pepped up. He's glad to have me for a date. He appreciates me. But that just hurts because it's such a contrast with Craig's not appreciating me.

Don's house is already crowded with kids. We walk in without ringing the bell or knocking. Nobody would hear us. It's that noisy. Lisa and Don see us and come over. They both give me a kiss on the cheek. Lisa is my friend, and so it's okay for her to do that. And I guess this is Don's specialty.

I'm already looking around for Craig. I almost hope he won't come. Then again, *I* haven't done anything wrong since the time he told me he'd call me and then he didn't. And besides, I'm wearing the beautiful white dress Mom finished for me just hours earlier. It looks so fresh and original and just about perfect. From now on Mom has a steady customer. Me. I'll be the only one in town wearing my own name on the back of my neck. Mom insisted on sewing in the label. It made her feel complete.

I see Craig from the back. And I see Eve beside him. So, it's true that he invited her. I knew it was, but seeing them side by side physically, not just knowing in my head that they'd be together, makes it real. Eve is dressed in diagonal yellow stripes. You can't miss her. I guess that's the point.

Jay gets us some food while I watch Craig and Eve dance together. They are both good dancers. I think Craig has caught sight of me. Now I feel awkward about my dress. I feel like a gleaming white swan, like I'm the trademark for Purity. After Craig and Eve finish dancing they walk over, holding hands. Jay comes back with the food at the same time. I don't know if Jay knows them, so I introduce everybody. Craig is dressed in a casual blue shirt and he looks terrific. Poor Jay. He has to try twice as hard to look half as good as Craig. I know the feeling.

But I've been underestimating Jay. He asks Eve to dance even though the yellow-striped dress she's wearing makes her look like a highway barrier you're not supposed to cross. She should have taken Mom's offer. At a thousand dollars it was a bargain. Eve is a theatrical type, and when her taste goes wrong, it goes *wrong*.

Craig is left with me. He stares at me coldly and doesn't say anything. I don't know why he came over in the first place. Probably it was Eve's idea.

Silence. And more silence. In the midst of all the music and talking and laughing in the room, there is a sharp and awful stillness between Craig and me.

I can't stand it anymore. "Why are you mad at me?" The words just come out.

Craig glares at me as if I'd just asked a moronic question. Glares and kind of smirks. For that one moment he doesn't look gorgeous. "Oh, come on," he says.

"Look, I don't know why you're mad at me."

"Sure you do. You did a great job for *Acne Magazine*. How many guys did you call from phone booths? That winner and champion, Renaldo. The one who bought you a steak dinner. How many guys did he beat out?"

"Now, wait a minute!"

"Hey, hey! Sounds heavy!" It's Jay. He and Eve have finished dancing.

Craig grabs Eve's hand, and they walk off.

"Are you two fighting?" Jay asks.

I just stare at him blankly. Then I say "Excuse me," and I go get Lisa and drag her away from Don.

"Okay, Lisa. You changed your mind about showing *Acne* around, didn't you? Now that it's gone down the drain and nobody is going to discover you, you decided to discover yourself. You've been showing off your article, haven't you?"

Lisa is mad. "First of all, Shari, I have a *right* to show *Acne* around. I didn't promise you that I wouldn't. But I didn't. And you know why? Because I got taken. I feel like an idiot, a jerk. *You* didn't get taken. *I* did. Remember the day we went to the city and found out the truth? When I got home, I dumped all my copies in the garbage can. They were picked up the next day. When I heard the garbage truck stop and their machinery grinding away, demolishing or compacting or whatever it does to trash, I felt reborn. I think I'll forever have a creepy reaction to acne when I see it. I mean, real acne on the skin, because it will remind me of those two degenerates, Derek and Bonita."

"Oh, Lisa." I want to hug her, but I don't want to make a scene. "I'm so sorry. Really, I'm so sorry."

"That's okay," she says. "We're both uptight about the whole thing. But why would you think I showed the magazine around? Is it in circulation around here? Be gentle when you answer, because the answer may ruin my life."

"Craig saw it. I don't know how."

"Ask him."

"I can't."

"I'll ask him."

"Maybe we don't want to know."

"Sure we do."

Don is staring at us, wondering what we're up to. He sees Lisa walk across the room to Craig. Don sort of shrugs to himself. He looks at me. I shrug, too. Don seems satisfied to have exchanged this gesture, as if it gave Lisa's mission an authentic aura of mystery. The room is so crowded that Lisa has to push her way through. I see her tap Craig on the arm and say something to him, and then Craig looks like he's excusing himself to Eve. Then he and Lisa walk to a corner of the room. At this point I wish I could read lips.

They talk for a couple of minutes. Then Craig goes back to Eve. Lisa walks toward me, triumphant. She has her answer. The answer comes to me at the same moment. Somehow Eve is connected to it. She saw the magazine and then showed it to Craig, knowing he would hate me when he saw the article. She had done something typically sly and nasty, and I can convince Craig that she has done this sly and nasty thing on purpose. Craig will be so mad at Eve that he'll forgive me. Justice has to triumph sometime.

"His *mother* showed it to him!" Lisa is almost cracking up, she thinks it's so funny.

"*What?*"

"His mother. Mom. The woman who gave birth to him. The one he remembers every Mother's Day."

"But how did she get a copy?"

"She saw the two creeps on TV. She thought they were refreshing. Couldn't you die? So she wrote to the station asking them to ask Derek and Bonita to send her a sample copy when the magazine came out. She got her sample copy. The rest, as they say, is history."

"What did she think of the magazine?"

"Pure crap."

Jay and I are one of the last couples to leave the party. I wanted to leave early, but he was enjoying himself. Why, I don't know. Because I was a total washout.

22

My father and Gloria Jean are getting divorced. It's the first smart thing my father has done since meeting Gloria Jean. He wrote this news to my mother. For once he didn't send a telegram. Mom doesn't care one way or the other. I think she's going to marry Gabriel. She raised the prices on her clothes twenty percent straight across the board, which was his suggestion. I like them together. It's comforting to see them bent over the desk working on cash flow. It's nice seeing him at our supper table sharing our casseroles. It would be great if he knows how to cook. I think my teeth are getting soft on casseroles.

Dad's moving back to town. He's opening up the kind of store he's closing down where he lives now. He's getting alimony from Gloria Jean. Lawyers are working on the divorce settlement, and Dad will supposedly be able to continue the kind of life he's become accustomed to living since he married Gloria Jean. I would imagine that's a rotten kind of life, but they mean it from a financial point of view. I guess Milton and I will be seeing Dad often. That's what Dad wanted that day in the kitchen. I'm looking forward to it without a tense feeling. So is Milton. Maybe my rash remark brought on the breakup of the marriage. But the marriage would have collapsed anyway. It's probably for the best that it happened now. Dad doesn't need any more horror stories to add to the ones he's already told Mom. I don't regret trying to apologize to Gloria Jean. You'd think I'd be kicking myself. But there are a lot of angles to every situation, and you have to go with the ones that you think are right at the time.

That's why I'm going to call Craig Andrew. I'm prepared for failure. Gloria Jean's "Wash your mouth out" prepared me. But it doesn't stop me. You do what you think you should do, and if it doesn't work out, well, at least you tried.

Lisa is with me all the way on this. She wants to be there when I make the call, but I tell her this is going to be a solo. "That's okay," she says. "You'll do fine by yourself. You'll be a smashing success."

The word *success* had been creeping back into

Lisa's vocabulary. She has made a fantastic recovery from the *Acne* disaster, and she's looking around for a new project. I shouldn't call *Acne* a disaster for Lisa, because she's been going out with Don. Her taste runs to Superman. There is an irony in all of this that has not escaped us. *Lisa* has met a gorgeous guy because of *Acne Magazine*. I may have struck out, but Lisa is firmly established.

"Well, here goes nothing," I say. I am in my usual hangout, Lisa's bedroom, and it's afternoon, and I'm about to go home and make my phone call.

Lisa has a final piece of advice. "Be cool. The more you want something, the less intelligent you'll be about trying to get it."

I know just where this sudden offering of wisdom has sprung from. It has come from the Lisa who had wanted to believe in Derek and Bonita. The Lisa who saw success written all over peeling walls and open wine bottles. It comes from the Lisa whose head wasn't screwed on quite straight when it should have been.

"Should we drink to your new philosophy?" I ask.

I'm trying to stall making the phone call.

"Why not," Lisa says. We go into the kitchen. Lisa takes a bottle of limeade and a bottle of orangeade from the refrigerator. She opens them.

141

"I'm green, you're orange. Okay?" she asks.

I gaze at the open bottles. Somewhere out there in the world, Derek and Bonita Prissamber are probably opening up a new bottle of wine to toast their latest enterprise, whatever it might be. If they didn't have more than a quarter of a million dollars in unpaid debts, I might wish them luck. I think Lisa learned something important from this whole "gorgeous guy" business, and maybe I will yet.

Lisa and I clink bottles.

23

It takes every bit of guts I can summon up to call Craig. I don't know how other people summon up guts, but I do it by telling myself that I'm a terrific person and then going into great detail about all the ways I'm terrific. I do this in private, of course. I give myself the gift of confidence. It's a gift with built-in obsolescence, and you have to use it during its brief life span. The last time I did this was when I called Craig from the pay phone. But I didn't know him then. It's easier when you're a stranger. You share only a remoteness and a blankness with the other person, and you can hide behind that.

I have a strong desire to make this call from a pay phone. This convinces me that there is something neurotic about me and pay phones and washing my hair before I make an important call. But these are small things to live with when you consider how bonkers the rest of the world is.

It's late afternoon. It was early afternoon when I decided to call Craig.

I dial his number fast. He answers. "Hello."

"Hi. Want to go for a walk?"

He knows my voice.

"Why should I?"

"Because if you don't you'll never know for sure if you're right or wrong about me. But if you take a walk, you'll know for sure."

He doesn't answer right away. I hope I don't sound like I'm begging or pleading. I have learned independence from my mother.

"All right," he says. "When?"

"Now."

"Now?"

"Now."

We say good-bye. I go and stand near the front door. All I have to do is wait for "now." A few minutes pass and I tell myself he's not coming and that's it. I won't call him back.

There's a knock at the door. That doesn't mean Craig's out there. It could be anybody. I refuse to have that leaping-up feeling of hope that is so miserable when it gets deflated. I open the door.

Craig is standing there. He's wearing the same

thick sweater he was wearing the other time we went for a walk. We both say "Hi" at the same time. I step out and close the door behind me. We start to walk. The same route as our last walk.

"Don't interrupt me," I say. And I start talking. "Okay, it's true that I was supposed to call a gorgeous guy for that *Acne Magazine* story. If it weren't for *Acne,* I never would have called you. I never would have had the nerve. I've seen you around school for a year. A year in which you never even noticed me, never so much as said hi."

Craig looks at me. Kind of quizzically. I add, "I know you didn't notice me."

Craig hesitates. "Well, it's a big school . . ."

"That's okay. I was going out, and I was having a good time. I wasn't pining away. But when the *Acne* thing came along, well, it was my chance to meet you. *You.* I did *not* call anyone else. I did not go out with anyone else. *You* happen to be Renaldo."

Craig stops walking. So do I. He turns and looks at me. I evade his eyes. I want to keep talking, to get it all out fast. "Derek, he's the editor, edited out Don and Eve to focus on the average girl and the gorgeous guy. And he changed a lot of details. Editorial license is what it's called. I didn't have anything to do with that."

At last Craig says something. "He had his nerve calling you average."

I feel a little shiver of happiness.

Craig is still looking at me. Then he says, "When I read the story in *Acne*, I pictured you standing at a pay phone, laughing while you phoned guy after guy. What was the pay phone all about?"

"I don't know. It made me feel more secure calling from there. Maybe it made me feel like I was conducting business instead of personally opening myself up to rejection."

Craig and I start to walk again. Neither of us says anything. Finally he says, "I feel awful. You know that, don't you? Don's party was a disaster for me too, but it was my fault. After I read *Acne*, I called Eve right up, I was so mad. The party wasn't even definitely on, but I was afraid I'd chicken out and invite you. I wanted to go with you."

I feel so wonderful, I clutch Craig's arm. I guess there really is something about him that inspires and even creates arm grabbers. We walk back toward my house.

I see Gabriel's car parked in front of it. I see him walking up my front stairs. "Do you like casseroles?" I ask Craig.

"Sometimes."

"Today?"

"Yeah, today." Craig grins.

We walk into my house. Milton is there, putting a casserole *back* into the freezer. Gabriel has brought steaks.

Craig calls home to say that he's eating supper at my house.

I watch him make the phone call. I love the sight and sound of it. I might even love him, but it's too soon to know. Craig is dialing the same number I once dialed to call him. *Twice* dialed. He's here because I made those two phone calls. I'm glad I did it, but I don't think I could ever do it again.

There must be an easier way to meet someone. Mom met her gorgeous guy through the Yellow Pages without even knowing she was doing it. Lisa met Superman through me. (Let's forget Lisa's moment of insanity when she thought Derek was a gorgeous guy.) Maybe Derek and Bonita should get the credit for my meeting Craig. And if the magazine had been a success, at this very instant girls all over the country might be marching up to telephone booths with their newly washed, squea..y-clean hair. I can just hear the deafening coast-to-coast clink of thousands of nickels and dimes being dropped into slots. The article would have done a lot for the telephone company and manufacturers

147

of shampoo. But maybe this isn't how you meet a gorgeous guy. Maybe you just live your plain, ordinary, usual life and someday he'll meet *you*.

Still, if you have strong nerves, and clean hair, it couldn't hurt to keep loose change in your pocket.

Meet Glenwood High's fabulous four, the

SENIORS

Kit, Elaine, Alex, and Lori are very best friends. Every girl's ideal, every boy's dream, these popular seniors share all their hopes, fears, and deepest secrets.

On the brink of graduation and adulthood, they're discovering themselves, planning for the future...and falling in love. Don't miss them!

by Eileen Goudge

____	TOO MUCH, TOO SOON #1	98974-4-13
____	SMART ENOUGH TO KNOW #2	98168-9-19
____	WINNER ALL THE WAY #3	99480-2-18
____	AFRAID TO LOVE #4	90092-1-17
____	BEFORE IT'S TOO LATE #5	90542-7-21
____	TOO HOT TO HANDLE #6	98812-8-27

Laurel-Leaf Books $2.25 each